LIGHT

SEARCH

BLACK
MIRROR

"A WILDLY ENTERTAINING RIDE RIPPED FROM
TOMORROW'S HEADLINES."
Eoin Colfer

When a young boy and his friends unwittingly
uncover a massive hoax while a tech-billionaire
hoodwinks people into believing that only he can
save the world – *who do you trust?*

First published in the UK in 2023 by Usborne Publishing Limited,
Usborne House, 83-85 Saffron Hill, London EC1N 8RT, England, usborne.com

Usborne Verlag, Usborne Publishing Limited., Prüfeninger Str. 20,
93049 Regensburg, Deutschland, VK Nr. 17560

ISBN 9781474991100 7145/1 JFMAM JASOND/23

Printed and bound using 100% renewable electricity at CPI Group (UK) Ltd CR0 4YY.

THE
LIGHT THIEVES
SEARCH FOR THE
BLACK
MIRROR

HELENA DUGGAN

USBORNE

CONTENTS

THE STORY SO FAR

1. THREE YEARS AGO AN EARTHQUAKE SHOOK THE WORLD LEAVING A BLACK MARK ON THE SUN. PEOPLE BELIEVE THE WORLD HAS SHIFTED OFF ITS AXIS.

EARTHQUAKE ROCKS WORLD

2. HOWARD HANSOM BUILDS THE TIPPING POINT ENCOURAGING VOLUNTEERS TO MOVE THERE. WITH ENOUGH WEIGHT IN THAT LOCATION THE WORLD WILL SHIFT BACK TO ITS ORIGINAL AXIS. EVERYONE WILL BE SAVED.

PEOPLE POWER
Become a Real Life
SUPERHERO

SOLAS WARNING

3. GRIAN'S SISTER SOLAS RUNS AWAY TO THE TIPPING POINT. GRANDAD GOES TO FIND HER.

4. MYSTERIOUS FIGURES IN BLACK CLOAKS SEARCH GRIAN'S HOUSE. HE FLEES TO JEFFREY'S HOUSE.

5. HIDING IN THE WILDE FOREST THE BOYS MEET SHELLI. SHE SAYS THE MYSTERIOUS FIGURES ARE PROCTORS. THEY BRING TROUBLE. THE THREE KIDS TRACK GRANDAD.

10. THEY DISCOVER THE HEAD OF THE PROCTORS ATTACKING HANSOM. THE CHILDREN SAVE HANSOM AND THE MAN IS TAKEN AWAY.

9. THEY ARE DISCOVERED BY HOWARD HANSOM. HE TELLS THEM THE MAN IN THE LONG COAT IS HEAD OF THE PROCTORS – A GROUP TRYING TO STOP HANSOM'S PLANS TO SAVE THE WORLD. HANSOM NEEDS THEIR HELP TO FIND HIM. HE PUTS THEM UP IN A HOTEL.

8. AFTER SEEING SOLAS ON A BILLBOARD EXCLAIMING SHE LOVES THE TIPPING POINT THE KIDS BREAK IN THERE TO FIND HER.

7. THEY SEE A MAN IN A LONG COAT LEAVING A NOTE ON A DERELICT PLATFORM.

6. WITH PROCTORS CHASING THEM THEY DISCOVER AN UNDERGROUND POSTAL RAILWAY AND FOLLOW IT.

11. THE KIDS DISCOVER SOLAS AND OTHER VOLUNTEERS LOCKED IN CAGES UNDER THE TIPPING POINT.

12. ON CCTV THEY SEE GRANDAD AND THE MAN IN THE LONG COAT LOCKED IN A ROOM. GRANDAD SAYS THE MAN IS VERMILION, A MEMBER OF THE COUNCIL OF COLOUR TRYING TO STOP HANSOM BECAUSE HE IS LYING ABOUT WHAT'S GOING ON.

HEROES

13. HANSOM THROWS A PARTY TO THANK THE KIDS FOR SAVING HIS LIFE. THE KIDS ARE HEROES. BUT THEY KNOW THEY'RE BEING SET UP.

14. THE KIDS RESCUE SOLAS AND SOME OF THE VOLUNTEERS WITH THE HELP OF SHELLI'S ANIMAL FRIENDS.

15. GRIAN SAVES GRANDAD AND VERMILION. THERE'S A HUGE EXPLOSION. SHELLI IS CAPTURED BY HANSOM.

20. THE BLACK MARK ON THE SUN GETS BIGGER – THE WORLD DARKER. GRIAN AND HIS FRIENDS MUST SAVE THE WORLD FROM HANSOM'S PLOT TO STEAL THE SUN.

19. GRIAN DISCOVERS THAT HIS DAD IS TAKING ANOTHER LETTER FROM THE WHITE ROSE TO THE COUNCIL OF COLOUR.

18. GRIAN RESCUES SHELLI. ON THE WAY BACK TO THE WILDE FOREST GRIAN FINDS A LETTER IN THE BAG. IT'S FROM THE WHITE ROSE, WHO SAYS THE SUN IS BEING STOLEN AND SETS OUT A WAY TO SAVE IT.

17. HANSOM ADMITS HE IS BEHIND WHAT'S HAPPENING TO THE SUN BUT SAYS THE WORLD WILL BLAME GRIAN FOR THE DESTRUCTION. HE DISAPPEARS ON THE HYPERLOOP, KIDNAPPING GRANDAD.

WANTED

16. GRIAN TELLS GRANDAD HE SUSPECTS HANSOM OF SETTING THEM UP. GRANDAD GIVES GRIAN A SMALL HESSIAN BAG, TELLING HIM TO TAKE IT TO THE COUNCIL OF COLOUR.

MAP OF
BABBAGE

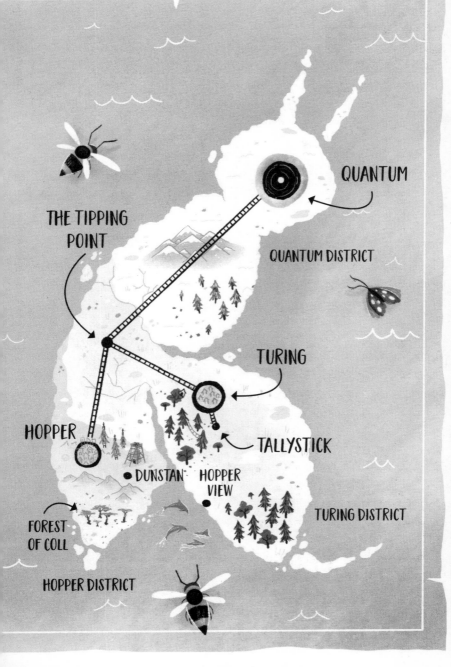

CHAPTER 1
DOOMED

"I am standing here a good distance back from the city, Mike," the woman said, speaking to the man in the brightly lit TV studio. "As you can see, fire and police officers are everywhere. No one is allowed in or out of the smart city. The Tipping Point was always a no-go area to everyone except those who selflessly volunteered to live here, but tonight, since what some are reporting as an explosion, security is even tighter and reporters are only allowed to stand outside these barriers behind me.

"The scene is eerily similar to those witnessed in Quantum, the capital city of Babbage, hours and days after the earthquake that rocked our world three years ago and left a black mark on our sun. I'll never forget the devastation I witnessed that day, the day that infamously became known as the Tilt."

The news reporter was shaking as she held the large microphone to her quivering lips. Her eyes were glassy as if she had been crying. Behind her, sirens raged, lights flashed and fires could be seen blazing in the distance.

"Though tonight, Mike, feels worse than three years ago. This time we know the black mark that appeared on the sun is a sign the earthquake tilted our planet into a precarious position. We know if this current unstable position is not fixed, the earth will, in the not-too-distant future, fly off into outer space and combust. We also know the Tipping Point and its creator – tech entrepreneur Howard Hansom – were our only chance of survival."

The reporter paused for a moment.

"I remember exactly where I was and how ecstatic I felt, after all the fear and hopelessness, the day Howard Hansom announced he had discovered how to save the planet. I remember the relief when he revealed plans to build his smart city, the Tipping Point, in the exact geographical location where if enough weight were applied, the world would tilt back into its correct position and save us all. And then I couldn't believe it when he declared he would create enough weight by paying people to move to his utopian city, full of his latest technologies, and effectively give ordinary people the holiday of a lifetime while turning them into real-life superheroes. It was the stuff of dreams, Mike; it was the storyline of a blockbuster movie.

"And now…now Howard Hansom, our hero, is missing presumed dead, and the Tipping Point – well, some say it can be rebuilt, that there may still be hope, while others say…they say we are doomed."

The man in the studio shook his head.

"And all the volunteers living in the Tipping Point – can you give any update on their situation, to family and friends currently watching this broadcast at home, Susie?" he asked after a few moments.

"No, Mike, we're not being told much. Hopefully we will be briefed soon. I have managed to interview a few people who were given special access to attend the earlier celebrations in the city tonight, prior to the explosion, but none were actual Tipping Point volunteers. No survivors have been found yet, but no bodies have been reported or recovered yet either…"

The woman looked away from the camera for a moment. Her eyes were watery when she looked back.

"And this deliberate destruction of the Tipping Point was carried out by children, Susie – am I understanding that correctly?" the man said a few moments later.

"Yes, Mike," the woman replied, as firefighters rushed past her. "That is correct. Grian Woods, Jeffrey Slight and a Wilde girl who we believe goes by the name Shelli – the very same children, who only moments before the explosion, were celebrated as heroes all over our screens for saving the life of Howard Hansom himself.

"Police don't think the children were acting alone though. They are believed to be members of a group called the Proctors, who have been trying to sabotage Howard Hansom and the Tipping Point since his plans to save the planet first came to light. The Proctors are a group of radical Tilt deniers who believe the planet hasn't shifted on its axis and that the earthquake was a hoax…"

"Huh – what an elaborate hoax that would be!" The man in the studio snorted, as the TV screen cut to pictures of Grian, and his friends Shelli and Jeffrey onstage earlier that night in the Tipping Point auditorium.

Grian huffed angrily and switched off Bob, his Hansom watch.

The news report was all lies.

CHAPTER 2

OUR SECRET

The treehouse Grian sat in belonged to the Wilde community, who had taken in him, Shelli and Jeffrey when they fled the Tipping Point earlier that night. The Wilde lived simply in the forest, in tune with the rhythms of nature. They didn't trust technology and, unlike almost everybody else in the world, they had never fallen for Howard Hansom's lies. Most people in Babbage thought the Wilde were weird.

Grian lay back on his beanbag, frustrated.

He wasn't just angry at the news report, he was angry with himself for daring to turn on his watch again. Because, unlike only a few days before, now he knew the truth: Bob wasn't his friend, and Howard Hansom and his technologies could not be trusted.

He had only turned on his watch because he had been desperately trying to reach his grandad again, when the news report flashed across his screen. On impulse he had swiped it open, then couldn't look away.

Grian knew the report was all lies, but he was sure most people would believe it.

He longed to go back to the time when he was like most people. When his watch was his best friend and Howard Hansom, the wealthiest and smartest tech entrepreneur ever, had all the answers and was going to save the world.

Grian's sharp learning curve had begun when his sister, Solas, ran away to the Tipping Point to help save the world, and his grandad, who had been minding them, went to find her. When Grandad never came back and black-cloaked strangers turned up at their house, Grian was forced into a dark adventure with his neighbour Jeffrey and a Wilde girl called Shelli.

The adventure led them to the Tipping Point and to the eventual discovery that the black mark on the sun hadn't been created because the earth had shifted on its axis, that the volunteers who had signed up to live in the Tipping Point had in fact become Howard Hansom's prisoners, kept in cages beneath his smart city – and that everything the tech entrepreneur promised the world was a lie.

And now, even though Grian and his friends had managed to save his sister and a few of the volunteers from Hansom's clutches, the situation was somehow worse than ever.

Grian's grandad was gone, kidnapped by Hansom and taken somewhere on his high-speed hover train, the Hyperloop, along with the rest of the volunteers who'd signed up to live in the Tipping Point. And the black mark on the sun had grown so big it now filled a quarter of its face.

You'll be the most hated boy in Babbage, Howard Hansom had promised Grian only hours before. And the man was right.

Grian's face, along with those of Jeffrey and Shelli, was all over every news channel, watch face, billboard and bus stop in Babbage and across the planet. All because of the false story of blame that the tech billionaire had concocted and spread through his Hansom-owned media networks, to divert attention away from whatever evil it was he had planned.

Solas, his sister, snorted loudly in her sleep, pulling Grian from his thoughts. She was curled up on a beanbag across from him, in the treetop hut swaying gently in the wind.

Grian felt for the small package in his pocket and pulled out the cream drawstring bag his grandad had given him in secret, just before he was kidnapped. Inside the bag was a piece of yellow rock crystal and a letter. The letter and crystal were from a mysterious person called the White Rose, who seemed to know what was happening to the sun and how to stop it.

Hansom was desperate to find this person too; so much so he'd kidnapped Grian's grandad, convinced he knew something.

Grandad had sworn he knew nothing about the White Rose, right up until he handed Grian the hessian drawstring bag. He made his grandson promise to tell nobody about it except a person named Yarrow, who was head of the Council of Colour, a group of academics, scientists and sceptics who refuted what Hansom said was true.

The letter revealed lots of details. Most importantly, though, it revealed it was one of four letters, and when all four were found the information they contained could help save the sun.

Grian glanced out the round window of the treetop hut at the moon, dreading the reminder the dawning sun would bring. He shivered and looked away, slinking deeper into his beanbag. His head swam in worries for both the planet and his grandad.

"What's that?" Shelli asked. His Wilde friend sat sleepily upright from her spot on the floor.

She nodded at Grian's hand.

Oddly, his left fist pulsed from a deep red to a subtle pink as he clutched the drawstring bag. Slowly he opened his fist.

A soft light throbbed from inside the bag.

"What's de light?" Shelli whispered, crawling over to his side.

Grian almost wrenched his arm away, before stopping himself.

He really wanted to tell his friends everything. To tell them the full truth of what had happened to him in the Tipping Point while Shelli was held captive by Hansom and Jeffrey was helping the volunteers escape. But if he told them everything, he'd be breaking his promise to his grandad to keep the White Rose's letter a secret.

But Grian knew he needed his friends, now more than ever. Grandad would surely understand he couldn't do this alone, not when the whole world was at stake.

"It's something grandad gave me...before Hansom took him..." he mumbled. "It's from the White Rose."

"Oh," Shelli gasped, in recognition of the name.

"I promised Grandad I'd keep it a secret, and now I'm breaking that promise!" he stuttered. "What if I never see him again... I've let him down already..."

"Grian, look!" Shelli nodded at his hand again.

The pulsing was quicker now and the light stronger.

Grian trembled, loosening the drawstring to peer inside. The small piece of cut yellow crystal shone brightly from within.

He emptied the crystal out onto his palm.

"Wow," Shelli gasped again, pulling something from her own pocket. "It's just like mine. I didn't think there were others!"

Grian looked at the familiar stick of rock crystal in Shelli's hand – she called it her Glimmer and had used it loads to guide them through darkness. The long hexagonal rock was a mix of jagged and smooth sides that shimmered in hues of purple and gold. But when it was activated, deep inside it a central circle of light beat like a living heart.

Then he stared down at the piece of rock in his own hand. Shelli was right: though much smaller and less regular in shape, this crystal was like her Glimmer.

"My Glimmer works when I think about someone I love – watch." Shelli was whispering, in case she woke Jeffrey and Solas.

She closed her eyes and bowed her head, her much larger piece of crystal sitting in her cupped palm. The Glimmer began to glow, and the glow grew gradually stronger until it highlighted both their faces as if they sat round a roaring campfire.

She shrugged, half opening her amber eyes. "I thought about Mam."

Shelli hardly ever mentioned her mam. All Grian knew was that she'd disappeared when Shelli was much younger. The Wilde believed the Proctors may have been behind her disappearance. Grian and the others now knew the Proctors were not some hooded gang opposing Hansom like the man had said, but that they were in fact his own private guards used to do his dirty work, so that Howard Hansom could double-cross the world while keeping his squeaky clean image.

"Oh," Grian said. "I was thinking about Grandad when this one lit up!"

"Well, maybe that one works de same way as mine then," Shelli replied, grabbing the crystal from Grian.

She waited for the crystal to stop glowing, then bowed her head again and closed her hand over it. A few seconds later her fist turned warm pink as an inner light shone through it.

"See." She smiled. "We should ask Mother! I thought my one was de only one ever made, but she'll know more. She gave de Glimmer to me when my mam went missing."

"No," Grian said firmly. "We can't tell anyone about it, or the letter. Grandad made me promise—"

"What letter?" Shelli asked.

"You have to promise," Grian pleaded, his cheeks red. He took the folded page out from inside the bag. "It's our secret – okay?"

He stared at Shelli until she nodded.

"Okay – it's our secret," she replied. "Just open it!"

"A secret?" Jeffrey said, sitting up on his beanbag. "I don't condone secrets. Unless, of course, I'm in on them!"

CHAPTER 3

A GLIMMER OF HOPE

The three friends sat in a tight circle watching the small piece of yellow rock crystal pulse in Grian's palm while he explained exactly what had happened that night after he'd left Jeffrey and Solas in the postal railway tunnel under the Tipping Point. "I'd rescued Grandad and told him my suspicions about Hansom. It was just before we went out into the warehouse where Hansom had you, Shelli." Grian shivered, the terror of the previous few hours washing over him. "That's when Grandad gave me this bag. It had been stitched inside his jacket... He made me promise to take the bag to Yarrow, the head of the Council of Colour, and not to tell anyone else it existed.

I opened it on the bus after we escaped the Tipping Point. When you were asleep, Shelli!"

"I wasn't asleep, I was knocked out!"

"What does the letter say?" Jeffrey urged, leaning forward.

Grian hesitated, swallowing a lump in his throat. "Grandad asked me not to tell anyone except Yarrow, but…"

"But we're not just anyone…" Jeffrey encouraged.

Grian half smiled – Jeffrey always had a way of cutting to the point.

His hand shook. Slowly he opened the letter. He coughed to clear his throat, and his voice trembled a little when he began to read out loud.

"Dear Adler,

I have made many mistakes in my life – the biggest was leaving you. But I can't hide behind my cowardice any longer. After a lifetime, I finally have the courage to suffer for the truth – I have to.

This is the first of four letters that I have sent out on your beloved postal network. Each of the others will be addressed 'Dear Postman' and in a red envelope. I chose the post as it is the only means of communication that cannot be hacked these days and because it's a proud profession built on discretion.

I hope you will understand, but for protection, I can't trust any one person with all of the information I have to disclose so I have split it up. Each letter will lead to a separate piece of a larger puzzle.

This crystal is the first of those pieces. When all the pieces are put together, they have the power to reverse the destruction I've unwittingly set in motion.

I have written the other letters as puzzles, just like the games we used to entertain ourselves with. This is not a game, though, Adler. I have written them this way in case they fall into the wrong hands. There are people who will kill if they get wind this information is out.

I know I am putting you right into the heart of this global deceit and in mortal danger, and for that I am sorry. But, if you are still the man I once knew, then you are still a truth-seeker and there is no other place you'd rather be.

If you need proof that what I write is real, then watch the skies. The black mark on our sun is just the beginning of this thievery – it will extinguish in phases until only the embers are left.

Once this phasing begins, time is running out. I beg you – find the letters, find the pieces, then come find me.

I have made it so I will not be able to go to you. I pray you know who I am, but I also insist it is vital you tell no one. If I am found and killed the final part of the puzzle dies with me and our world as we know it is no more.

My resistance is based on the power of love and now you
have all of mine – please keep it safe.
You are my glimmer of hope.
The White Rose."

Grian's two friends sat speechless. Only the faint whistles of Solas sleeping slipped through the hut.

"That doesn't sound promising," Jeffrey uttered, breaking the silence. "The information in the letter must be true – the White Rose clearly states if we need proof that what they write is real then we must look to the sun. And it is extinguishing in phases.

"First there was the black mark, after the earthquake three years ago, and then it extinguished further this morning. The sun is a quarter black now! How long before only the embers are left? From everything I've read, and I'm widely read, life on earth is impossible without the sun. I'm not an avid geography or biology buff, but I'm quite sure we're in tremendous trouble, and by we, I mean every—"

"Stop it, Jeffrey!" Shelli said. "Panic is useless. De letter proves de White Rose is real. And they know de sun's being stolen and—"

"Yes, yes, you're quite right! How could I miss that. The sun is actually being stolen," Jeffrey exclaimed. "Of course – that is precisely what 'thievery' means. And if I understand that letter correctly, then the White Rose appears to have also been involved in this thievery. How else can one interpret the line – 'the destruction I've unwittingly set in motion'? Though it is obvious they regret their involvement!"

"It has to be Howard Hansom stealing the sun," Grian said. "But why would he? Like Jeffrey just said, we all need the sun to survive. It makes no sense – I mean, he lives on this planet too!"

"Stop, both of yous. We can't worry about why, right now," Shelli said anxiously. "Don't ya see, yous are getting distracted – just like Hansom wants us all to be. De White Rose has sent three more letters out in de post. If we find those letters and solve de puzzles, we'll find de pieces they lead to. We can fix de sun and save de world. And de letter says we have de first piece already – that crystal. And your dad has another of de White Rose's letters, Grian, your mam told us that this morning."

Shelli was right. In the midst of everything, Grian had forgotten his dad had another letter.

His mam surprised everyone, including Grian, when she'd told them earlier in the Wilde meeting hut that she and his dad were part of a group called the Postal Network who were already looking for the White Rose's letters.

Grian's dad was the head postman in the Turing District of Babbage, and his mam explained how a while ago Grandad asked him to look out for three red envelopes in the post addressed Dear Postman. His dad put word out with trusted members of the postal service and they'd formed the Postal Network and begun looking for the letters.

Grandad also told Grian's parents that if any letters were found and he himself went missing, they were to take those letters to the Council of Colour. His parents were at a Postal Network meeting discussing the recently found letter when they heard of Grandad's disappearance. So that's what his dad was doing right now – bringing the letter they'd found to the Council.

"We just need to find de Council of Colour, Grian, and give them your granda's letter." Shelli interrupted his thoughts. "They'll have de other letter too, soon, if not already. We'll be able to help them look for de next piece of de puzzle."

Shelli was right; surely this meant hope.

"Perhaps we should tell Mother or your mam about your grandfather's secret letter, Grian. The imminent end of the world is a rather big deal to hide from them?" Jeffrey added.

"No." Grian shook his head. "Grandad made me promise not to tell anyone. The White Rose makes him promise too. With his technology, Hansom knows everything. We can't risk him finding out about this. It's our secret now, promise you won't tell anyone."

Shelli nodded, her face serious. "I promise, Grian."

"Of course – I'll be the soul of discretion," Jeffrey answered cryptically.

Grian never understood why Jeffrey couldn't just use normal words.

"So where are de Council?" Shelli asked.

"I don't know," Grian said, shaking his head. "Grandad never told me."

"That makes it a little more difficult to find them," Jeffrey replied. "If only we could access the hNet. There must be something online about the Council's whereabouts?"

"No," Grian snapped. "We can't go on the hNet or—"

"But I just saw you check your watch!" Shelli eyed him suspiciously.

Grian hesitated.

"Okay...right... Well, yes. I just checked Bob because...well, I gave an hSwarm to Grandad before he got on the Hyperloop with Hansom."

Grian and Jeffrey had first seen the hSwarms in the small equipment room off the underground warehouse where Solas and the other volunteers were held prisoner in the Tipping Point. He had never heard of hSwarms before that, but Jeffrey had been blown away when the pair discovered them.

Because insects and invertebrates were dying out all over the world, Jeffrey explained that Hansom had designed hSwarms to replace them and do their work. But since discovering what Howard Hansom was really like, Grian knew the hSwarms' greatest powers were covert. They made the perfect tiny spy.

"Genius – utter genius giving your grandfather an hSwarm. Of course, it's something I would have done myself…" Jeffrey exclaimed.

"Thanks." Grian shrugged. "Grandad messaged through on the hSwarm app on my watch a while ago. The signal was fuzzy, but he said he was in a city somewhere and there was a strange sky. That's all I could hear before it cut out."

"A city somewhere? And a strange sky," Jeffrey mumbled, his brow creased.

"I know it's hard to hear, Grian, but there are bigger things now than saving your granda. If we don't save de sun, no one will survive!" Shelli said bluntly.

Grian's heart sank but he knew Shelli was right. Grandad had given him the letter and told him to find Yarrow. He had been a Tilt denier and was a truth-seeker – like the White Rose wrote. He knew Grandad would say exactly what Shelli had.

"You're right," he admitted. "The sun is dying and this letter says we can help stop it. We need to find the

Council of Colour. Once we've saved the sun, then I'll save Grandad... Maybe I could ask Mam where the Council are; just pretend I'm curious or something – she has to have an idea, if Dad's on his way there now?"

"If you ask her specific questions, she'll know we're up to something," Jeffrey stated. "Adults have quite suspicious minds."

Grian walked back to the window and looked across at the warm light in the Wilde meeting hut a few trees away.

"Maybe I don't have to directly ask her. They're still in the meeting hut. I could go there now and say I couldn't sleep. That I'm scared or something. I bet Mam'll let me stay. And maybe they'll say something about the Council while I'm there. Any information will help!" he said, turning back to his friends, an idea slowly forming.

CHAPTER 4

MOTHER

Shelli snuck out first, Grian just behind her. It was decided Jeffrey would stay in their hut in case Solas woke up.

The sharp cold bit Grian's skin as he stepped out onto the platform, which swayed gently, high in the trees of the Wilde forest. Now that the sun wasn't warming the days as much, the nights grew colder too.

He shivered, pulling the hood of his jumper over his head before tightening the strings at his neck to shield off the bitter air.

Grian looked across through the sea of branches and rope bridges, past the numerous treetop homes to the lights in the distant meeting hut.

Mother and the Aunties and his mam and some of the rescued volunteers had been in there talking for hours now, and Grian imagined they'd be hours more.

Mother was the leader of the Wilde and also Shelli's grandmother. The Aunties, a group of older women, were Mother's advisors. They met regularly in the meeting hut to talk about Wilde things, like the running of the tribe.

Suddenly, Shelli leaped from the platform out onto a set of the hanging rings that dotted the forest and were used as a quick method of transport through the treetop town, for those brave enough. His friend swooped forwards into the darkness before tumble-turning like a gymnast onto a platform a distance away.

Her Glimmer lit the sky like a firefly as she waved it through the air, directing Grian towards her.

A slight sweat broke out on his brow. He gripped the thick bristly sides of the rope bridge that swayed beneath him. He was glad it was dark. The darkness meant he couldn't see the distance below or the huge black mark on the sun – a constant reminder of the task they faced.

"We'll fix the sun, Grian," Shelli whispered, icy clouds forming round her words when he caught up to her on the next platform. "And we'll find your granda. I feel it, and my feelings aren't ever wrong."

Grian didn't know what to say as he followed her onto the next rope bridge. Shelli seemed so certain, but he wasn't. He tried hard not to think of the size of the task; the whole thing seemed too big.

"Maybe your feelings are wrong this time," he replied at last. "Things are bad, Shelli. Without the sun... And we're just kids..."

"We're not just kids! And anyway, Mother says kids can do anything, and I know she's right 'cause we just did so much. We rescued your sister and all those volunteers and found out Howard Hansom's a liar. We even found a way to stop him. We just have to keep going. We have to fight for our future, Grian, and we're good at fighting."

"But...why can't we leave it to the adults?"

"Because most adults are scared to see de truth. But we're not, we're fearless. We need to show de adults what's real and what's possible – then they'll join us... Your granda knows you're a kid and he still gave ya that letter," Shelli said, her amber eyes on fire in the light of her Glimmer.

Grian was about to reply when she shushed him. They were outside the meeting hut now.

"Come in. I was expecting visitors," Mother called from inside.

Grian's stomach did a flip as Shelli pushed open the door.

Surprisingly, Mother sat alone in the middle of the round room, on a colourful mat. Her long white hair hung in a plait round her shoulders and her eyes were closed. Her legs were crossed and her palms rested upright on her knees. She was sitting just as she had been the first time Grian met her in the meeting hut.

"Sit down." She gestured to the mats on the floor around her before opening her cold blue eyes. "De universe told me to wait up tonight. It said I had something very important to do. I was just trying to figure out what that might be when you two showed up – so maybe you're it."

"I don't think we're very important," Grian joked nervously, as he sat down on the floor.

"So why are you two here then?" she asked, her voice soothing. "And don't lie to me, Shelli – you know better than that."

Mother couldn't see very well but, just like Shelli, she had a strange way of knowing things.

Shelli blushed as Grian looked anxiously across at her.

"Ahem, I couldn't sleep…" Grian replied, turning back to Mother. It wasn't really a lie.

"Now, I might not have great use of these eyes but that doesn't render me blind, Grian. Since you've come back, you're burdened. There's a heaviness on your shoulders, a responsibility you're carrying?"

He blushed now too and looked at Shelli again. His friend shrugged.

"Ahem…maybe. I'm not sure," he responded, feeling flustered.

"You can't tell me, and that's fine," the old woman replied. "But whatever it is you need to ask me to make this burden lighter to carry, just ask. We all have our part to play in de unfolding of our times, Grian, and I can sense your part is vital. I will help you in whatever way I can."

"Ahem…okay… Well, ahem…I was wondering how to get to the Council of Colour. I mean, if someone wanted to find them, how would they?"

Mother laughed, and Grian's face reddened further.

"Well, de Council are not all in one place; their members are in hiding throughout Babbage. But if someone did want to find de Council, they would need to speak to Yarrow, de Council head. Go to de Forest of Coll, to our Wilde tribe there. De group leader is Fiach. Tell him Mother sent you and that you need to speak to de Council. Ask for Amergin, their Seer – I'm sure he will have already had a vision of you coming."

"Oh great… Thanks." Grian tried to sound confident as goose pimples dotted his skin.

"And go tonight, before de forest wakes. I won't tell anyone you've gone, and I'll pretend this conversation never happened."

"But Mam will…"

"Don't worry about your mam. She's a strong woman and she'll have Solas with her. This task has been given to you, and I believe its completion is vital to all our futures…"

"But how do we get to the forest?"

"Follow de road south out of Tallystick and cross de strait to de Hopper district at Hopper View. It's de quickest way. But stay out of sight. You're wanted now. And not just by de police, they might be de least of your worries, ordinary people will be looking out for you too. They're angry, they're told their only hope of a future has been robbed and you three are to blame."

Grian sat on his hands as they started to shake. "But we don't know what we're—"

"None of us know what we're doing, Grian – that's a secret us grown-ups never tell you. Take your time, and listen to your heart. It will direct your head. Above all, don't give in to fear – fear keeps de mind confined."

Grian closed his eyes and tried to listen to his heart, as Mother had just said. But all he could hear was the jumble of thoughts that raced through his head. His stomach twisted itself into a knot. What if he couldn't do it?

"It takes time, Grian. But children can access their hearts much better than adults, and that will make you fearless. I was a thousand times braver as a child than I am now. When I was very young, me and my two sisters ran away from a cruel man and built a life of freedom for ourselves here in de forest. At times we had no food or shelter, and I felt like giving up, but we helped each other through. And look at what we built…"

"But Shelli's brave, and Jeffrey too. I'm just not sure I am." Grian stuttered out the words that came from a place deep inside.

"I was brave because I had to be – there was no choice," Mother continued. "You will be too. And just like me and my sisters, you three will pull each other through."

"You never really speak about when you were young, Gran," Shelli whispered.

"Because it's painful to remember, pet. But it's also something I am very proud of, and it's something I sense you two need to hear right now."

"My Glimmer," Shelli said, taking it from her pocket. "I heard one of your sisters made it… Is that true?"

Mother wavered a little before looking across the room to a section of the huge decorative hanging that wrapped the wall of the whole meeting hut. It told the story of the Wilde. Weaved into the part of the tapestry where Mother seemed to stare unblinking were three young white-haired girls sitting in the middle of the forest, as animals danced around them.

"Yes. Adabelle, my youngest sister, made it. She was quite clever," Mother replied, tears welling in her eyes.

"Did she make any other Glimmers?" Shelli asked.

"No. She disappeared a long time ago – before you were born, Shelli," Mother replied, then quickly changed the subject. "Now, there isn't much time before de forest wakes. Pack your stuff and go. Follow de road south to Hopper View and cross de channel there. I will pretend I never saw you. And take de bikes, Shelli."

CHAPTER 5
DÉJÀ VU

"How did Mother know all those things? It was as if she could read my mind," Grian whispered, as they made their way back across the rope bridge.

"Well she can, sort of," Shelli replied. "I've told you this before. When you tune in, you can do anything. We all can. Animals do it all de time, people have just forgotten how."

"Tune into what, though?" Grian asked, confused.

"Life...or energy. It's not something I can explain. You have to feel it first, then you'll know!"

They stopped outside their hut and Shelli slowly pushed open the door, so as not to wake Solas. Jeffrey sat straight up.

"Well, did you find out anything useful?" he asked, looking hopeful.

"We did actually," Shelli replied, smiling. "We're going to de Hopper district."

"Hopper?" Jeffrey exclaimed, before lowering his voice again. "In south Babbage? But there's nothing of note there."

"Nothing of note! Only mountains and forests and rivers and a great big desert..." Shelli rattled off.

"Nothing of importance, I mean," Jeffrey corrected himself. "Though perhaps that's precisely why the Council chose it. I'm presuming the Council of Colour are there?"

"There's a Wilde tribe there in the Forest of Coll. Mother said they will help us find the Council," Grian jumped in, before Shelli could pounce on Jeffrey.

"So you told Mother?"

"Not exactly. She just knew I needed to ask her something. So I asked her how to get to the Council. She told us to leave tonight, before everyone wakes up!"

"But we've only just got here, and Hopper is quite a distance to travel. Can't we at least take advantage of a few hours' sleep?"

"De sun is dying, Jeffrey!" Shelli's hands were on her hips now. "And we're not going de long way. We're going down de coast to Hopper View and crossing de channel.

Mother says it's a much quicker way to get to de forest. She even told us to take de bikes. Come on, we haven't got much time. We need to move now."

"By 'bikes' I hope you mean electrically propelled bikes," Jeffrey said, looking a little worried.

Solas shifted on the beanbag.

"What are you three talking about?" she groaned, not even opening her eyes.

Grian shook his head rapidly at his friends. "Nothing, Sol, just, ahem…just talking about nothing really," he said.

"Grian Woods, I know when you're lying." His sister's eyes sprung open and she suddenly sounded like their mother.

"Just go back to sleep, Solas."

"I'm the oldest here, so you have to tell me what's going on! Otherwise I'll go right now and tell Mam," Solas said, sitting upright.

Shelli growled and backed towards the door to block it.

Solas looked straight at Jeffrey.

"There's something up, isn't there, Jef?" she said, her tone now softer.

Jeffrey squirmed, blushing a little under the pressure.

"We're leaving for Hopper tonight," he blurted as if releasing a valve.

"I knew it!" Solas stared glared right back at her brother. "Are you going to find Grandad?"

"No… I can't tell you, Solas – I made a promise. Just stay, please. Mam needs you here. If we both go she'll have no one."

"Just tell me what you're doing! Don't you trust me, Grian?" His sister looked upset now.

Solas was stubborn, which was probably why she'd run away to the Tipping Point in the first place. If he didn't tell her, she'd do everything possible to find out what was going on – including telling their mam or following them.

Grian sighed. He knew he could trust Solas; that wasn't why he hesitated. Partly it was because he didn't want her involved – he'd almost lost her once and he didn't want that to happen again. Also, Grandad had told him to keep his secret and now he'd already told two people and was about to tell a third. But it was Solas, and it wouldn't be fair if he left her out. Even though most of his life he kind of thought he hated her, the last few days proved his mam had been right all along: they were brother and sister, and it was a bond stronger than anything.

He took a deep breath before quickly filling her in on the whole story.

"So we're going to find the Council and give them the White Rose's letter, like Grandad told me to," he finished.

"And it's not that I don't want you to come, Solas, it's just, well, Mam needs someone here and, ahem… It's just, I…I thought I was never going to see you again, and then we got you back, you're so tired and weak, and I…I just don't want to lose you again."

Solas looked down and fidgeted her hands for a minute. When she looked back up, her eyes were glossy.

"Thank you," she sighed. "For telling me the truth and for…you know…for everything."

Tears rolled silently down her cheeks and she rubbed them away with the back of her sleeve.

"I suppose someone does need to cover for you three with Mam and the Wilde." She shrugged, half smiling now.

"Come on," Shelli whispered, glancing out the round window as a faint line of morning light seeped into the dark sky. "The forest will be awake soon."

Solas stood up, slow and stiff as if she was an old woman. It was a stark reminder of how only the day before she'd been locked up and half-starved in a cage below the Tipping Point with the rest of Hansom's volunteers. She looked fragile as she followed the threesome out onto the hut platform.

"How do I get messages to you if I need to?" she asked. Her teeth chattered and she wrapped her arms tight around herself to combat the cold.

"Talk to de animals," Shelli replied. "They'll get de message to me."

"But I don't know how to…"

"Just talk normal, like ya are to me." Shelli smiled, before disappearing over the edge and down the ladder cut into the side of the thick tree trunk that was home to their hut.

Jeffrey turned and gave Solas a hug and an awkward wave before following quickly after Shelli, climbing down towards the forest floor.

"I need to go now too," Grian said, his stomach in knots.

"Just be careful, please," Solas whispered, wrapping her arms around his neck and burying her head deep into his shoulder.

He hugged her back with all his might and wished more than ever that everything was normal again.

"I will, I promise," he mumbled into her hair.

Then he eased himself from the hug and looked into his sister's eyes one more time before slipping over the edge of the platform and down the ladder to his friends. Landing with a soft thud on the ground, he looked up and saw Solas's dark shape disappear back inside the hut.

"This way," Shelli ordered.

Nach, her fox, had appeared out of the forest and now stood loyally at her side.

With only the glow of her Glimmer, Shelli weaved nimbly in and out of the large trees that packed the dense forest. Grian followed behind, ducking now and then to avoid the scrawling branches that somehow seemed to always reach for his face.

Eventually Shelli stopped, at what appeared to be a large mound of leaves.

"Give me a hand," she whispered, leaving the Glimmer down by her feet.

Under the soft light, Grian could see that the mound was actually a green tarpaulin covered in a mesh of sewn-on leaves. He grabbed the edge of the rough material as Shelli instructed, and together they pulled it off to reveal a selection of bicycles, all with baskets and panniers, propped upright in a wooden rack.

"Oh dear," Jeffrey gasped, inspecting the bikes. "All these are self-propelled, just as I feared!"

"We use them when we need to go shopping in Tallystick. They'll get us to Hopper View faster," Shelli said, grabbing the handlebars of a pale-blue bike with a brown wicker basket.

"That may be true if I had indeed learned to cycle," Jeffrey replied, "but unfortunately for us and the current situation we find ourselves in, I had much more pressing things to do with my time."

Shelli shook her head, looking more than a little shocked.

"You really don't know how to cycle?" she asked, irritated.

"I'm afraid not – no." Jeffrey answered.

"Ahem, okay... I'll give you a backie," she replied, patting the metal carrier that rested over her rear wheel.

"Excuse me...a 'backie'?" Jeffrey furrowed his brows in confusion.

Grian laughed as he grabbed a bottle-green bike and listened to Shelli explaining what was probably one of the only words Jeffrey didn't know.

Once they were ready Shelli picked up her Glimmer and dropped it in the basket of her bike, before wheeling the bike forward through the rough forest terrain. They wouldn't be able to ride until they reached the road.

The bikes were heavy and it was a struggle to pull and drag them over and around tree roots and rocks in their way.

Grian relaxed a little when they eventually found their way on to the well-worn track that led through the trees towards Forest Drive, which was an estate that ran beside the forest on the edge of Tallystick – Grian and Jeffrey's home town.

As the day dawned, it felt almost like déjà vu.

Grian had been here before, heading off from the Wilde forest with Shelli and Jeffrey. The first time, though, they had barely known each other. They were just looking for his grandad, without a clue of how serious things would get.

This time they were under no illusions. This time they knew they had a world to save.

CHAPTER 6

A WOBBLY START

They'd been pushing the bikes for a while along the worn path when they reached the edge of the Wilde forest. Shelli stopped just inside the cover of the trees and held up her hand to stop the others, before ducking out onto the road to check the coast was clear.

Grian peered through the thick branches out onto Forest Drive. The estate was bathed in dull street lighting that turned everything a shade of orange.

Because of all the terrible stories he'd heard about the Wilde, Grian had been afraid to go into the forest before he'd met Shelli. But now the forest felt safe and out there, Tallystick, felt like the scary place.

"Right, you're the tracker," Grian addressed Shelli, as

she popped back in through the trees. "So where are we going?"

"That's not how it works, Grian. For tracking to work I need to have something to track," she huffed, a little annoyed.

The air was so cold their small circle was shrouded in clouds of breath that hung like see-through mushrooms over their heads.

"If only I could just turn Betty's hMaps on for a moment to locate Hopper..." Jeffrey sighed.

"No, Jeffrey!" Grian snapped, sounding angrier than he'd meant. "I already said we can't risk Hansom tracking us."

"It wasn't a desire I was going to follow through on!" Jeffrey tutted. "It was just an observation on how simple life was before..."

"Hand over your watches," Shelli said, nodding at the pair. "It's too dangerous, and if yous don't have them ya won't be tempted."

Grian hesitated as he stared down at Bob.

What would his wrist even look like without his watch on it? Bob felt part of him, like an extra arm. What if they got in trouble and he needed to contact someone? What if Grandad tried to get in touch again through the hSwarm? What if... There were so many what ifs.

Jeffrey appeared stuck too, as he rubbed his finger affectionately across Betty's screen.

"Okay – since none of yous seem able to take those things off," Shelli said, leaning her bike against a tree. "I'll do it for ya!"

Grian grimaced as she grabbed his wrist and unbuckled Bob before doing the same to Jeffrey.

Nach began to claw out a hole in the forest floor, and when it was ready Shelli dumped the watches inside.

"No… What are you…" Grian yelped, feeling suddenly sick.

"What we should have done ages ago," she replied, piling the loose earth back on top of the devices.

Grian squirmed and looked at Jeffrey, who appeared frozen stiff, his face as white as Howard Hansom's teeth.

"Now use your brains, if you have any left!" Shelli smiled, stomping down the dirt in satisfaction.

She seemed to be getting a bit too much enjoyment out of this, Grian was thinking, when a light turned on in one of the houses opposite and snapped him out of his despair.

"We need to get going before we're seen," he whispered, pulling back a little further into the forest. "People are waking up."

"The Hopper district is not a popular or populated place, so perhaps, once there, we don't have to worry so much about being seen?" Jeffrey said, the light clearly pulling him out of the shock of losing his watch too.

"Outside of the city, it mainly comprises of a few small towns for the people who mine the desert. I remember learning about its mining history in school. The towns looked like something from antiquity. I doubt the people there have the latest Hansoms. They're probably only using hOS12. Although…we don't have the latest Hansoms now either…"

"Mine the desert?" Grian asked, surprised. "I thought deserts were just full of sand!"

"Oh no, there are lots of minerals in the desert, and if I had Betty I'd be able to list them all. In fact, the metals are a must to build most of Hansom's technology. Silver, gold, platinum and palladium, as well as earth metals such as yttrium and gadolinium, lanthanum and neodymium…"

"Not sure you really need Betty," Grian joked.

"Mother said to follow the road to Hopper View then cross the channel there," Shelli interrupted, eager to get going.

"Oh yes, of course – we're going via the channel at Hopper View! That's a quaint seaside resort on the coast. It's not far from here," Jeffrey said. "You can actually see Hopper from the beach. We holidayed there many times on holidays when I was younger."

"So do you know the way, Jeffrey?" Shelli replied.

"Thankfully I have a photographic memory." Jeffrey

smiled. "We take the road out by the hForest and then it's straight the whole way."

"Is it far?" Grian asked, heaving his bike out of the forest onto the road.

"Perhaps an hour – in a car," Jeffrey answered.

"That must be like a whole day on these," Grian gasped, feeling a little sick.

Shelli didn't say anything as she pushed her bike out onto the road and pointed at the metal carrier behind her. Jeffrey grimaced, climbing aboard before holding onto the back of the saddle in front of him.

"It's not very comfortable," he complained as Shelli pushed off.

"Then we'll just have to go fast!" she laughed, cycling away.

Grian pushed his foot down on the pedal and the bike launched forward. It had been a long time since he'd cycled, though he wasn't going to admit that to Shelli. He wobbled from side to side for a bit before finally finding his balance.

The sun had almost fully risen as they pedalled through the quiet streets of Tallystick. There wasn't a cloud in the morning sky, though Grian never would have known it if he hadn't looked up. The larger black mark that now covered quarter of the sun meant the daylight was dim and dull, as if a huge storm was brewing.

It wasn't long before they were out of the streets of Tallystick and onto an open road that was lined either side with hForests. These were huge areas full of digital towers designed to look like trees.

Grian's grandad went mad when the hForest in Tallystick was built, because it meant they cut down most of the existing forest, leaving only a few real trees mixed in between the fake ones so the digital forest fitted more seamlessly into the landscape.

Grandad and the Wilde were some of the only people who were angry when hForests started to appear in Babbage. Everyone else had been delighted, because the real trees disrupted signals and the fake ones that replaced them enabled all Hansom's technology to connect and communicate with each other much faster.

"The digital trees are quite realistic up close, aren't they? You can't really tell the difference, except for the buzzing," Jeffrey mused, his hair brushed back by the wind as they sped along the road.

"I can tell de difference and so can de animals," Shelli replied, not looking at all under pressure as she pedalled. "De real ones give us oxygen! Ya do know they cut down lots of real forests for these fake ones?"

Grian was about to reply, when he bristled at the sound of a distant siren that was quickly growing louder. He wobbled a little looking over his shoulder. Behind him, lighting up the sky at regular intervals, were flashes of blue.

"The police," he shouted ahead to Shelli. "They're coming this way!"

"Just act normal," Jeffrey roared back. "Pretend we're just three innocent children on a cycling trip."

"You didn't see the news reports, Jeffrey. If they recognize us we're finished," Grian panted heavily, as he tried to catch up to the other two.

Without a word, Shelli swerved her bike off the road into the hForest.

"Oh my! Ouch! Aghh! Shelliiiiiiii," Jeffrey rattled out, bouncing up and down on the carrier as they careened over the bumpy ground.

"Grian, we need to hide!" she yelled back.

Grian ducked into the hForest after them. His shoulders, arms and hands shook as he gripped onto the handlebars and flew across the rough terrain. The bike slowed as the going got tougher, and when his legs couldn't push any more, he finally admitted defeat and jumped off.

He knew hForests buzzed a little because he'd heard the sound before whenever he passed any, but now he was inside one the buzz was much louder and kind of irritating.

"We'll be quicker on foot," he shouted, hiding his bike in a dip behind one of the digital trees.

"Some of these trees are real," Shelli said, after abandoning her own bike in the same dip. "I think we could climb them."

She jumped for the low hanging branch of a real tree nearby and began climbing up squirrel-like, before wrapping her legs around a thick branch and leaning back down to reach out for her friends.

"Grab my hand," she shouted, as the sirens grew louder still.

Jeffrey jumped for her outstretched palm but couldn't reach.

Thinking quickly, Grian fell to his hands and knees and formed a bridge. He braced his back as Jeffrey stepped up and jumped for Shelli's open hands. She grabbed him and pulled while Grian stood up and pushed, until Jeffrey struggled onto the branch beside their friend.

Then they both reached down for Grian. Though he tried as hard as he could, he could only jump high enough to reach the tips of their fingers. Quickly he scrambled about, looking around for something he could leverage himself up with, when suddenly blue lights penetrated the forest. The police car had stopped on the side of the road a little distance away.

He watched, terrified. Two police officers stepped out.

Grian's heart pounded. He raced to hide behind a

thick, buzzing tree trunk. He could almost feel the electricity shooting through its plastic bark as he watched the police walk slowly through the hForest.

The two men wore familiar-looking black gloves.

One of the policemen's Hansoms beeped.

"The children were spotted on Tallystick security cameras about a half an hour ago. Comb the hForest for them. Word of warning, our detectives have just finished speaking to some of Hansom's security team – they told them these children are highly dangerous, so take care. Also, be careful with the hThoughtTech gloves on loan from the Hansom corp – none of you have been fully trained in their use yet and we don't want any more destruction."

"Noted. We've just arrived in the hForest. If they're here, we'll find them. I'll make that my business. They may only be children, but they've stolen my child's future," the larger of the officers replied, tapping his hEarPods as he stepped slowly round the trees.

Grian felt sick. The police were wearing Hansom's hThoughtTech gloves.

"They're...they're after us," Grian stuttered. He looked up at his friends perched on the branch above. "I'll never get up that tree. I need to go..."

Grian first saw the hThoughtTech gloves, boots and visors in the small storeroom under the Tipping Point where they'd also discovered the hSwarms only a few days before. Jeffrey said the equipment was part of Hansom's latest policing technologies and explained all the cool things they could do by harnessing the energy of the air just by the wearer thinking about it.

But when Grian had worn the gloves himself in the Tipping Point while taking on the Proctors, and felt their immense power in his fingers, it kind of scared him. With one flick of a wrist, he could have killed someone.

"Follow Nach!" Shelli ordered, as her fox darted off in the opposite direction to the approaching police.

Grian hardly took a breath as he raced after the fox cutting swiftly through the hForest. He was sure that at any moment his clumsy movements would give him away and a blast of energy from the gloves would wipe him out.

Suddenly Nach skidded to a stop by a mound of stones that appeared to mark the entrance to a small underground tunnel. The fox clawed at the ground in front of the entrance, which was dotted in what looked like animal poo. Then she ducked her head and walked into the tunnel before quickly coming back out. She whimpered and repeated the same actions again and again while staring intently at Grian with her deep brown eyes.

"No... You don't want me to hide in there, do you?" Grian panted, eyeing the dark pit in front of him.

Nach whimpered again.

"Grian Woods, are you out here? Jeffrey Slight? I'm

sure you're all scared. Maybe you didn't know what you were getting mixed up in when you joined the Proctors. We don't want to hurt you. Just give yourselves up and we can sort all this out," one of the police officers called.

Grian couldn't see him, but the policeman didn't sound far away. It looked like his choices were prison and the end of the world, or swallowing his fear and shimmying down this tunnel.

Quickly he got on his hands and knees and crawled into the tight, dark space.

The top of the tunnel was wide enough to squeeze inside, but it quickly grew narrower as he descended. Grian tried to calm his panicked breath as the clay sides tightened in around him. The buzzing of the hForest grew fainter as he wriggled, wormlike, on his stomach head first down the sloped ground until his body was almost inside. He stopped moving when the space became too tight, which he was sure left his feet exposed – he could feel a slight breeze at his ankles. Then something plonked onto his lower legs and blocked any remaining light that trickled inside. Fur tickled his skin where his trousers had ridden up – was Nach lying on his feet?

Grian lay motionless. He closed his eyes and tried to think about anything else but the cramped space and lack of air.

We're going to save the world, we're going to save the

world, he repeated over and over in his head, until his racing heartbeat slowed.

That was when he noticed the stench for the first time. The place really stank – the smell dug inside his nostrils and reached for his stomach, almost making him retch.

Next a low growl met his ears. The growl was weak and rattly, but it was still terrifying. Alongside the growl were faint whimpers, like those of the newborn pups he'd met in his cousin's house once.

He squeezed his hand into his pocket for the small cloth bag and pulled out the rock crystal. Thinking of his grandad, he held it in his palm. A small glow filtered out from the object and lit the earth walls of the tight tunnel.

Scattered on the ground in front of him were fragments of bones, feathers and eggshells, and a little ahead, at the end of the long sloping tunnel, was a small grey creature with a black and white striped head. He thought it was called a badger, if he remembered right from school. She lay on her side, feeding three young cubs.

The tiny things weren't moving much, except for the odd whimper. On each intake of breath he could see their delicate ribs. The mother was hardly moving either. She looked miserable, tufts of her grey coat missing in patches. Although she snarled, she seemed fragile and weak, unable to do anything about her surprise intruder.

After a while the badger appeared to settle and she relaxed into her feeding. Somehow Grian relaxed too, mesmerized by the way the sick mother nuzzled and nurtured her hungry babies.

He was engrossed in watching the family when the weight lifted off his lower legs and light filtered down the tunnel again.

Someone grabbed his ankles and he squirmed in panic as he was yanked roughly back up the slope, out into the hForest. Half blinded by the light, he tried to scramble away as his eyes adjusted and saw Shelli looming above him. Their bikes lay in the tufted brown grass behind her.

"Get up," she ordered. "The police are gone. We need to get moving!"

"Oh, Grian… There is a whiff of something unsavoury coming off you." Jeffrey wriggled his nose as he bent down to inspect him.

"But…ahem…" Grian stumbled over his words. "There's a badger family in there. A mother and three babies. They look sick and hungry…"

"Most of their home is a digital forest. Of course they're sick, Grian! Their shelter is gone. Their food is gone too – there are no buds or fruit on fake trees. Whatever insects are left can't live in these plastic things either. All de animals in these places are sick. They have been for a while. That's how I got Nach," Shelli said angrily. "Her mam and sister had already died. Nach was de last of her family left. She was a tiny cub when I found her."

Grian looked at the sky so his friends couldn't see the tears that welled in his eyes. The sun had risen further. It must be nine or ten in the morning now, but it didn't feel like that. The day was still dull and grey, reflecting his mood.

"Isn't there anything we can do?" he almost pleaded.

Shelli shook her head as though frustrated, before closing her eyes.

A few minutes later a squirrel appeared in the tree above her and softly popped down onto her wild red hair. The small animal bowed its head, and Grian could swear it closed its eyes for a moment too, before coming back to life and dashing off into the forest.

"He'll tell Mother and someone will come to save de badger and her cubs. Nach will wait here with them until help arrives. She won't be able to cross de channel de way we're going anyway, so she'll follow after us by land. Now come on, let's go."

"Maybe we don't need so many hForests," Jeffrey mumbled as they pushed their bikes off through the fake trees, leaving Nach behind curled up at the mouth of the tunnel.

They walked in silence for a while, keeping to the

cover of the hForest until eventually they stepped out on to a narrow road.

After looking around for any sign of the police, they mounted their bikes. Grian and Shelli cycled for a while longer listening to Jeffrey moan every time they hit a bump. Eventually they reached the top of a steep hill. Grian was exhausted but breathed a sigh of relief when he saw the road on the other side wound down to a small seaside village.

"There it is," Jeffrey announced. "Hopper View."

CHAPTER 7

HOPPER VIEW

They left their bikes in a ditch and walked down the road towards Hopper View. Grian breathed in the sea air and his shoulders relaxed. Until now he hadn't realized he'd been holding them up round his ears. His lips tasted salty and it brought back memories of holidays with his family, eating salted fudge and ice cream. His shoulders stiffened again; these were memories he didn't want or need to have right now.

From their vantage point, he could see colourful seaside houses, painted in bright blues, yellows, pinks and greens that made up the village. The main road wound up past a stone sea wall that overlooked the beach below. A small ramp gave access down to the soft sand, that Grian imagined on a normal hot summer's day would be filled with half-dressed bathers. A restaurant beside the sea wall was packed with people having breakfast, and a police car was parked on the road just by it.

"Everything looks as I remember," Jeffrey said. "Except for the police presence."

Grian gulped and his heart thumped. Among the holidaymakers having their morning coffee he could see police walking table to table, asking questions.

The threesome kept their heads down. As they got closer to the village a man and woman stepped out of a doorway just behind them. The pair were talking in hushed tones.

"The news said Hansom still hasn't been found." The woman sounded scared.

"He's dead, darling," the man replied. "I expect it's a body they're looking for now. It's tragic. I do hope they find whoever is behind that awful explosion and lock them up."

"Don't say that about Hansom," the woman scolded him. "He was our only hope. What will happen to us all... to the world?"

"I don't know," the man replied, "but let's not think about it now, darling. We're on holiday."

Grian stopped and let the couple pass, not wanting to hear any more.

"Going into the village centre seems risky," Grian whispered, as they stood a little back beside the main car park. "Everyone is on edge and we'll be spotted. There could be security cameras too. That's how the police in the hForest knew we'd been in Tallystick."

"We just need to get to de sea so we can cross de channel," Shelli replied. "Is there a way to get there without going into de main village?"

"Yes, if we continue up that way," Jeffrey replied, pointing to a road that wound up a small hill to their right. "We'll circumnavigate the village to the boat harbour."

As they walked up the hill they passed a row of thatched cottages. Grian spotted a clothes line full of beach wear, blowing in the morning breeze.

"What if we looked like we belonged here..." he whispered. "Nobody would notice us then – we'd blend in with the other kids."

"What are you suggesting?" Jeffrey asked, raising an eyebrow.

Grian nodded towards the clothes line filled with wetsuits and towels.

"The wetsuits will definitely come in handy crossing the channel," Shelli said.

"Yes. How exactly are we going to achieve that?" Jeffrey asked distracted. "It's been playing on my mind. Even if we did manage to commandeer a boat, I'm not sure we could master it. Unless either of you have seafaring experience?"

Grian ignored his friends and peered over the wall towards the clothes line. The house seemed quiet, the curtains still closed in most of the rooms.

With a hint of guilt, he took a deep breath, jumped the wall and raced across the cut grass to the line. His heartbeat quickened, pulsing loudly in his ears. He grabbed three wetsuits, all varying sizes, and a few beach towels before sprinting back to his stunned friends.

"Wow! That took guts, Grian!" Shelli smiled proudly, patting him on the back as he handed over the wetsuits.

"I wouldn't normally condone stealing but in this case I think it's justified," Jeffrey stated as he took his suit.

"Come on," Grian urged. "We need to find somewhere to change."

"I've just the spot," Jeffrey said, racing ahead.

The road passed by a small stone round tower perched on the cliff, overlooking the sea. Jeffrey slipped down a narrow laneway behind the tower to a public garden, where the three friends hid behind a large bush with a sea view and quickly got changed. Grian was sweating by the time he'd wrestled on the wetsuit.

"I certainly think we look the part." Jeffrey smiled, reaching round to pull up the long cord at the back of his suit, fastening the zip.

Jeffrey was right. In their new gear, they did look like normal seaside kids about to head for a swim. Shelli fitted almost perfectly into the smallest wetsuit. Grian had forgotten how birdlike she was hidden beneath the large clothing she normally wore. His suit was a perfect fit too, though Jeffrey's was slightly loose but not enough so anyone would really notice.

Grian grabbed one of the towels and flung it around his neck in an effort to hide his face, as Shelli filled her rucksack with their clothes.

"Right, let's get to the harbour," Grian said. "Did you come up with any ideas about how we're crossing the channel?"

"Yes." Shelli smiled without adding another word.

"She won't tell us," Jeffrey replied. "I expect she thinks we won't like the answer."

As they made their way back out of the public gardens onto the road, Grian spotted a group of children in wetsuits, chatting and laughing a little ahead. The group was led by a man in board shorts and a life jacket. He seemed to be some sort of instructor.

"Come on," Grian said, rushing after them. "I bet they're heading to the harbour – we'll blend in."

The threesome sped up and slipped in at the back of the group.

"I can't wait for today's lesson," one of the kids in

front said to their friend. "Mam says I'll be the best sailor in the class!"

The group were passing a large grocery shop when a police car drove slowly past them. Grian shivered as he looked away.

"Act natural!" Shelli hissed, as the group turned off the main road down a steep slope towards the harbour.

They stopped at the bottom of the hill beside a bunch of docked sailing dinghies.

"Welcome to the first day of summer sail camp!" the instructor announced as the group spread out around him. "Now that you're all here, let's get straight to business. For any of you who don't know, these dinghies behind me are beginner sailing boats and this is what you'll be learning to master over the next few days..."

"Will the big mark on the sun affect the sea?" A little girl quivered, as she raised her hand into the air. "My sister told me it would and I'd be swallowed up by a giant wave if I went out on a boat."

"No, it won't affect the sea." The boyish instructor seemed a little nervous too though he kept a brave face.

"But my sister said—"

"Is your sister a scientist?" the instructor interrupted, looking slightly frustrated now.

"She's eleven. She likes football..."

"So she's not a scientist," the instructor continued.

"Why don't we leave the sun to the scientists, and we'll get on with our sailing. I'm sure everything will be fine, so let's just have some fun!"

A few children gave cheers of excitement, while others looked nervously about.

Grian felt for the small cloth bag he'd stuffed inside his wetsuit when he got changed. He suddenly realized that if he went into water the letter would get wet, and then no one would be able to read it. He spotted a white plastic bag stuck on a thick rope that tied a fishing boat in place nearby and scooted over to pull it off. The bag smelled of fish. He grimaced as he popped the cloth bag inside the plastic one before knotting together the plastic handles.

He stuffed the bag down the neck of his wetsuit and moved back to his friends just as the class began to head towards the dinghies.

"Three or four per boat," the instructor called.

"I think we should slip off now," Shelli whispered.

Grian was about to agree when he spotted three police officers standing on the footpath high above the harbour. They were glaring down at the group.

"Don't leave yet," he whispered to the others, heat rising in his face. "I think we're being watched. Act normal, as if we're meant to be here, and get on the boats like everyone else."

His heart thumped as they moved in line towards the top of the group. He glanced back over his shoulder. The police were heading down the slope. Surely they'd seen them.

Grian panicked, forgetting their plan to act normal. The line was moving too slow. They needed to move faster. He elbowed past the kids in front waiting for the next boat. Shelli followed, forcing Jeffrey forward as he apologized loudly to everyone he jostled past.

Grian scrambled clumsily onto the small sailing boat as some kids protested behind him. Then he turned and pulled his friends on with him.

"What are ya doing?" Shelli exclaimed, stumbling onboard. "I thought we were meant to blend in?"

"Hey, stop them! Police!" a policewoman roared, running down to the harbour just as the instructor launched Grian, Shelli and Jeffrey out into the waves.

"Stop. That's them! They're those kids who destroyed the Tipping Point!" she cried at the instructor, who seemed frazzled as he looked from the boat back to the officer.

"Stop, you three, or I'll use these!" She was addressing Grian and his friends now, as she held up her black gloved hands.

The policewoman was wearing Hansom's hThought-Tech gloves, just like the police officers in the hForest.

Grian stumbled forward. He thought his heart might burst as he grabbed clumsily at the sail rope trying somehow to move the boat faster. They had to get away. They couldn't get caught.

The policewoman stopped at the water's edge and closed her eyes before thrusting her hands powerfully forward.

"Duck!" Grian cried out, just as a large wall of water rose up from the sea to tower above their little boat.

He barely had time to scream before the weight of water crashed down on top of them and the boat splintered to pieces.

CHAPTER 8
AT SEA

Grian's arms and legs felt like a rag doll's in a washing machine as the sea pulled him round and round. Everything was a blur and the muffled sound of gurgling and distant muted screams filled his eardrums. He caught a flash of Jeffrey's leg, then of Shelli's hair, like strange red seaweed in the murky blue waters.

He struggled to the surface to gasp in air, before the waves dragged him back just to swirl him round and round again.

His lungs ached underwater. He wanted to open his mouth and suck in even the tiniest bit of air, but something deep inside begged him not to, just before the world went black.

Then he saw Solas and his mam and dad and grandad, and he stopped struggling. They were in their sitting room, playing a game. It was Christmas and Grandad had gotten a new puzzle that kept everyone guessing for hours. Grian felt warm and happy as he slipped towards the bottom of the sea.

Suddenly he was jerked from his cosy Christmas gathering, as something pulled on his wetsuit and without warning he was zipped across the sea, just below the surface. He could see the sky rippling above him. The sun, even in its diminished state, was beautiful as its light rained down like crystals on the water.

Seconds later, something smashed against his shoulder. He turned to see a large orange ball bobbing beside him. He grabbed the thick rope that wound round the centre of the ball and broke through the surface, gasping for air.

After a few minutes of coughing and spluttering, he looked around. He was hanging onto a large orange buoy in the middle of nowhere, far out to sea with no sign of the shoreline.

"Shelli, Jeffrey!" he cried and cried, his voice travelling in all directions across the huge expanse of blue.

His breath grew ragged and he'd already begun to tremble when a large protruding fin appeared above the water a distance away and a dark shape sped just under the surface, straight for him.

"Shark, shark, shark!" he screamed to no one, as he tried to clamber up onto the large orange buoy, which kept spitting him back into the sea.

Suddenly, the creature swerved and Jeffrey burst from the water, smacking up against the side of the buoy. Grian grabbed at his friend's wetsuit just before he slipped down beneath the waves once more.

"What happened?" Jeffrey spluttered, moments later, gripping firmly to the buoy rope.

Grian was just about to speak when he noticed two protruding fins swimming in wide circles round them. His heart pounded. He nodded towards them, unable to form any words.

"Oh my," Jeffrey cried. "Do you think we're dinner?"

Grian's terror was interrupted by the distant sound of laughter. The laughter rippled across the sea, growing gradually louder until he spotted Shelli sitting upright in the water as if riding on top of the waves. She was speeding towards them while holding tight to another grey fin, her flaming red hair flying like a flag on the wind behind her.

"Watch this!" she cried.

Bending forward, she appeared to wrap her arms round whatever creature was in the water beneath her and disappeared under the waves.

"Shelli!" Jeffrey gasped.

The waters stilled. Grian's chest tightened as their friend didn't re-emerge.

What felt like ages later, though it was probably just moments, there was a huge splash as a large grey creature emerged from the sea jumping in an arc above their heads. Shelli screamed in excitement, clinging to the smooth-skinned animal.

"I'm sure that's a dolphin," Jeffrey shouted, as Shelli disappeared beneath the waters once more before popping to the surface on the other side of the buoy.

Their friend pushed herself up to sitting and shifted the mass of wet curly hair from her face before smiling over at Grian and Jeffrey.

"So yous have met my buddies," she called, as the dolphin brought her towards them before stopping an arm's-length away.

Shelli held onto the creature as it popped its grey head above the surface. Its long bottle-like nose and small black eyes seemed almost to be laughing while it made a series of whistle and cackle sounds.

"I'd already asked de dolphins to bring us across de channel," she explained. "I just didn't think they'd have to rescue us first..."

"What exactly happened back there?" Jeffrey asked, still holding tight to the rope wrapped round the buoy. "I saw the police officer running, and then I vaguely remember a huge wave before everything becomes jumbled…"

"She was wearing hThoughtTech gloves," Grian spat, now trembling with anger as much as the cold. "She made the wave…"

"But that technology hasn't been handed over to the police yet. As far as the wider world knows, Howard Hansom said his policing technologies were still in testing phase."

"I heard someone talking through one of the policemen's Hansoms in the hForest. They said that the Hansom company had loaned the technology to the police but that they had to be careful because they weren't trained to use it yet," Grian growled.

"Clearly," Shelli huffed, rubbing the dolphin's nose as it cackled away beneath her. "That woman nearly drowned us! But on de plus side, with any luck de police and everyone else might think we're dead now and leave us alone."

"We may well be dead soon if we don't get out of this bitterly cold water," Jeffrey chattered, his lips a shade of blue.

"You're right, let's go," Shelli replied, closing her eyes.

A few seconds later the two dolphins who'd been circling the buoy swam over towards them.

"Climb on and hold tight," Shelli called, before jetting off across the waves.

A dolphin pulled up alongside Grian and cackled, gesturing its nose towards its fin. A little nervous, Grian let go of the buoy and splashed over to the animal.

"You won't go too fast, will you?" he whispered, shivering.

The dolphin clicked and whistled as if laughing, as Grian grabbed its triangular fin and struggled onboard. Then he gripped the round sides of the dolphin with his legs and held on tight.

Immediately the animal zipped off. Grian coughed, swallowing a wave of the salty sea that splashed up into his face. His heart felt like it was about to explode. He started to laugh. At first it was nervous laughter, until the feeling took him over and he was laughing from somewhere else, somewhere deep inside, a place he'd almost forgotten lately.

Jeffrey and Shelli began to laugh too as they flew through the waves parallel to him, until all three of them were in hysterics dashing across the vast sea like jockeys in an invisible horse race.

The wind whipped through Grian's hair as the sea slashed his face. Though the world seemed to be falling apart, he felt more alive than he ever had in his whole life.

After a short while he could see land. His dolphin slowed when the sea grew shallow, until the sand was clearly visible in the waters below. The dolphin stopped, and reluctantly Grian let go of its fin and slipped off. He was belly-button deep in the water and still giggling.

Then the dolphin nudged his left hip with its nose. Grian was confused when the creature hit him again and began to wave its tail in the sea, almost like a dog, before swimming in circles round him.

"Do you want to play?" Grian smiled as he lunged across the water for the animal, starting a game of chase.

Shelli, Jeffrey and their dolphins joined in and they played for what felt like ages. By the time they'd bid goodbye to the animals, who quickly disappeared back into the rolling waves, all three were exhausted, and Grian's stomach and face ached from laughing.

"That was amazing…" he gushed, stepping over a mass of seaweed as they headed towards the sandy shore.

"Ya know humans hunt them," Shelli remarked.

"No way. We don't hunt dolphins!" Grian exclaimed, feeling suddenly sick.

"Their meat is a delicacy," Jeffrey stated. "And though it might seem cruel, it is necessary that we hunt them to lower the competition with fishermen. It's simply survival of the fittest, from Darwinian evolutionary theory!"

"Survival of the greediest you mean," Shelli huffed.

"No, I can't… I don't…want to know." Grian shook his head. He was shivering now and didn't fancy getting into a spat. "We need to keep moving."

The beach in front of them was empty and vast. Its yellow sand stretched as far and wide as he could see. And just at the back of it was a towering wall of green.

"Look, the forest," he panted, running now to keep warm. "That must be the Forest of Coll! Let's find the Wilde and they'll lead us to the Council. Once we've saved the world we can think about saving the dolphins!"

CHAPTER 9

FIACH

Grian ran towards the vast forest that scaled up the side of what looked like a huge mountain. The air in the Hopper district was much warmer than Turing where they'd come from and he started to feel a little hot and sticky in the stiff wetsuit.

His heart thumped as adrenaline coursed through his body. He'd almost died, and he decided he didn't want to die. Not ever.

Somehow what happened in the sea made everything clearer.

An energy grabbed him now, unlike anything he'd ever felt before, and he knew what he wanted to do. Up until now he wanted to save the world for his family and friends, but now he wanted to save it for the badgers he'd met in the hForest and the dolphins who'd just rescued him in the sea. Shelli was right, and suddenly it was as though Grian had known it all along: the world wasn't just for him and his friends, it was for everything, from the tallest of trees to the tiniest of insects.

"Ya're starting to understand it all – de bigger picture – aren't ya?" Shelli winked, slowing as they approached the forest edge.

Grian smiled and looked away. Maybe he was.

"Are we sure this is the right forest?" Jeffrey asked, breaking through the treeline.

"As far as I know," Shelli answered, looking cautiously around. "It's de main forest in de Hopper district. It's huge and covers most of de Hopper mountains on this side. On de other side of de mountain is de desert."

"Let's hope we don't have to venture there," Jeffrey said with a shiver. "I've read many terrifying adventure tales about people expiring in deserts."

"We won't have to. Mother said the Wilde tribe we need live here in the forest. We just have to find them," Grian replied.

"I'm betting they find us first," Shelli said, before opening the rucksack still strapped to her back and taking out their clothes.

"They're wet." Jeffrey grimaced, holding his trousers aloft.

"They'll dry fast out here," Shelli said, sitting down to pull off her wetsuit. "De sun might be gone out a bit, but I bet Hopper's still hot. And it's better than walking de mountain in these stiff things!"

The three friends took a few minutes to get dressed before heading off. Their pace slowed as the dense forest grew darker. Grian looked up and couldn't see the sky through the nest of branches above. The trees were so tightly packed it was hard to get by them without being scraped.

He felt nervously for the small bag he'd tucked back into his trouser pocket. He'd kept the plastic wrapped round it and was afraid to take a proper look in case water had gotten in and ruined the letter.

"Shush," Shelli whispered, holding up an arm as she stopped dead. "I think we're being followed."

Grian stepped on a large twig and quivered as it cracked loudly beneath his shoe.

He jolted in fright, as a sharp cry rang through the trees around them. It sounded like a wolf howling. Grian's heart pounded. He glanced in the direction of the sound.

"Does this forest have...have wolves?" he muttered.

"It's possible," Jeffrey whispered, looking a little spooked himself. "Wolves are quite common in the Hopper district."

Another howl echoed round them, mirroring the first.

"Mother sent us," Shelli called out. She sounded fierce and stood tall. "We're looking for Fiach!"

A deep drum beat through the forest, the vibration pounding Grian's chest. He and Jeffrey pulled close together, almost back to back, and watched the trees as Shelli fearlessly stood her ground. The branches around them began to rattle in fury. Grian held his breath.

Numerous figures stepped forward through the thick branches to form a tight circle round the threesome.

Half of the figures in the circle were human, but every second position was taken up by a four-legged animal with a scruffy grey coat and wild eyes.

"You see, wolves are quite common here," Jeffrey whispered again.

"How do we know Mother sent you?" a deep voice bellowed.

Grian stepped back and his eyes darted round the circle looking for a way to escape. He'd thought the Wilde here would be friendly, like the ones in Tallystick.

"Ask Amergin, your Seer. I am Shelli – Mother's granddaughter, Aoife's daughter. We need to see Fiach. Fast."

A man stepped inside the circle. Like all the other Wilde around them, he was dressed in rough black trousers and a shirt, over the top of which was a strange sleeveless jacket made from what looked like black feathers. He was barefoot.

"I'll take you to Fiach," he said.

Then without another word the circle opened, and the man turned and walked back through it. Grian looked at Shelli as she stepped forward to follow.

"Are you sure?" he hissed quietly, pulling on her sleeve. "They don't seem very friendly."

"Just come on," she hissed through gritted teeth.

"I have a feeling that we may have little option, Grian," Jeffrey added, following Shelli.

Grian looked at the ground, avoiding the eyes of those in the circle as he too stepped through.

The surface beneath him softened as he walked, and he soon realized that, though well concealed, they were following a hidden forest track covered in a thick carpet of soft moss.

They'd been trailing the Wilde man wordlessly for a while when he signalled for them to stop. Then the man took two large leaps forward and jumped into a hole in the ground before, seconds later, flying straight up into the sky as if he'd sprouted wings. He then somersaulted into the dark canopy of trees high above them and disappeared.

"What?! Wow – how'd he do that?" Grian gasped, looking skywards. "And where did he go?"

The treetops were a maze of criss-crossing branches, and it was hard to understand how the man could have slipped through them uninjured.

Shelli lit up her Glimmer and scanned the area at their feet where the man had just sprung out from, but there was nothing there.

"I wonder if it might not be a rather large and concealed slingshot system of some sort," Jeffrey pondered as he moved to his knees to inspect the ground.

He pulled back what appeared to be a sheet covered in a layer of moss that camouflaged the hole so well it was very hard to see and revealed a large circular pit dug deep into the ground. Strung across the centre of the pit was an extremely wide rubber band strapped to the middle of which was a huge piece of leather about the size of the top of Grian's kitchen table.

"I expect he jumped on that leather pad," Jeffrey pointed, "and his weight counteracted the rubber band to propel him upwards into the trees. Quite clever – though obviously primitive."

"Primitive!" someone laughed, high above them, just before a dark shape shot down into the pit like a missile and quickly somersaulted back out, landing without a sound on the soft forest floor beside them.

"I'm Fiach," the man addressed Shelli. "Now who exactly are you?"

CHAPTER 10

THE NEST

Fiach's weathered face scowled, as if he'd much prefer to eat the three friends for breakfast than help them. Grian was all of a sudden less afraid of the wolves skulking somewhere in the forest behind him than he was of this man.

Fiach was broad, square-shouldered and -jawed, and wore the same black feather vest as the other Wilde people they'd just met in the forest.

"I asked a question. Now answer it!" He glared at Shelli.

"I'm Shelli, daughter of Aoife and granddaughter of Mother Wilde. Mother sent us here to find you." Shelli sounded much more confident than Grian felt.

"I had heard we'd have visitors, but I didn't think we'd have them this quickly. We had lookouts posted in de desert. How did you slip past them?"

"We didn't come that way. We came across de channel. De dolphins helped us. There's no time to waste, so it was much quicker that way," Shelli answered, looking slightly smug.

"So what do ya want with me?" Fiach shifted, for the first time looking uneasy.

"We don't want anything from you exactly," Grian started, stepping forward.

Grandad had set him the task, he needed to be brave now.

"And you are?" Fiach eyed him seriously.

"I'm, ahem, Grian Woods, son of…ahem…" He wasn't sure how to make himself sound as impressive as Shelli just had.

"Son of Cam and Saoirse Woods, and I am his neighbour – Jeffrey Slight." Jeffrey extended a hand towards the man.

Fiach snarled. "These boys aren't Wilde. There's a whiff of de city off them." He nodded at Shelli, ignoring Jeffrey's outstretched palm.

"Yeah, but they're my friends," Shelli said, sounding frustrated.

"Is there somewhere we can go, somewhere private?"

Grian interrupted, checking over his shoulder. "I'll tell you everything then…"

He didn't want to say a word about the Council out in the open where anyone could hear them.

The square man turned and walked away through the trees without another word. Shelli huffed angrily and followed.

Jeffrey looked uncertain until Grian walked forward too.

Fiach moved like an animal through the forest, so silent and quick it was hard to keep up. Then he came to a sudden stop by a thick tree.

"Quickly, climb the stairs and when you get to the top say the word oscailt," Fiach explained, looking cautiously around before moving towards the tree.

Grian watched in amazement as the man then pulled open the knotted bark like a cupboard door to reveal a set of carved wood steps spiralling up through the middle of the hollow trunk.

"Oscailt, like 'open' in Wilde tongue?" Shelli asked.

"Yes. Go now," he urged, almost pushing them up. "We don't use this entrance much and we don't want anyone to know about it."

"But wherever are we going?" Jeffrey asked, craning his neck to look. "It's just a jumble of branches up there."

"Stop your talking and go now," Fiach replied. It was an order this time.

Shelli was first to set off, Grian and Jeffrey following behind, winding their way up the middle of the tall tree. At the top of the stairs they stepped out onto a long narrow wooden platform.

On one side of the platform was a sheer drop to the forest floor far below. Grian wobbled as his head spun at the dizzying height. Afraid he might fall, he stepped back and reversed straight into a towering wall woven out of twigs, leaves, branches and moss. The wall was so high it was impossible to see over and so dense it was impossible to see through. The nest-like structure appeared to run to the left and right of Grian as far as the eye could see, as if it wrapped round the top of the whole forest like a ribbon.

"There's nothing up here." Grian shivered, trying to ignore the sheer drop just feet away.

"Oscailt!" Shelli said beside him.

Suddenly a section of the wall in front of them opened inwards like gates, revealing that the platform they'd been standing on was part of a much larger floor area. Two people dressed in the same black clothes and feather waistcoats stood sentry at each gate. They beckoned the children forward, then closed the wall behind them.

"Well I n-never…" Jeffrey stuttered in awe.

Grian was in awe too as he looked around. They were in some sort of a town in the trees. This town wasn't like the one in Shelli's forest, though, where homes were built in individual trees and linked with bridges and you could still see the forest floor.

This Wilde town was built on a single wooden platform that appeared to span over the top of the whole forest, which probably explained why it was so dark on the ground below. The enormous platform was pockmarked with holes cut to accommodate the trees that grew through it everywhere so that at this height, the huge trees looked like saplings.

Hanging from branches of the trees everywhere were large teardrop-shaped cocoons also made from a weaving of twigs, moss and leaves. The cocoons hung in clusters and most of them were just big enough to fit one person inside, though there were larger ones too. All were lined in soft blankets and some had people snuggled inside, sleeping.

"They're beautiful – just like weavers' nests," Shelli whispered, her eyes wide.

"What's a weaver?" Grian asked, trying to take it all in.

"A songbird – they weave their nest."

"Hence the name, I imagine," Jeffrey noted.

"Follow me," Fiach ordered as he appeared out of nowhere, landing softly on the platform in front of them.

He turned and walked away without another word. The three friends followed behind in stunned silence, mesmerized by the new world they found themselves in.

As they walked, they passed through an open kitchen in the middle of the platform. A large sail of cream canvas-like material was pulled taut over the top of the kitchen, shielding it from the weather. A small group of people were cooking up delicious-smelling food in large battered silver pots that hung over round metal firepits. Grian's stomach rumbled, reminding him he was starving.

On one side of the open space was a long table that appeared to be made from a full-length slice of a tall tree. It was longer than any dinner table Grian had ever seen and looked like it'd fit at least one hundred people on the wooden benches that ran down both sides.

A little further on from the kitchen they passed by a mini forest of treetops, their branches decorated in the same woven cocoons they'd seen earlier, only these ones were much smaller and were dripping in all sorts of fruits and vegetables that grew inside them. Lots of people busily tended to the cocoons; some climbed across the treetops picking the fruits and vegetables, while others seemed to be sowing seeds or watering younger plants.

Shelli gasped. "Wow, what a food garden... Wish ours was this good!"

"We've a better climate," Fiach answered bluntly. "It's much easier to grow food here than it was in de Tallystick Wilde forest. We'll soon be able to feed all de Wilde tribes in Babbage from this base."

94

"Not if the sun disappears," Jeffrey thought aloud.

Fiach ignored him as they continued onwards, passing through what looked like an outdoor school and then a library until they reached a set of round wooden huts. They were similar to the ones in Shelli's forest, but these huts were built directly on the platform.

"We can speak privately here," Fiach said, stepping into one of the huts and closing the door behind them.

Hanging in a circle from the ceiling of the hut, facing each other, were about ten woven teardrop-shaped seats. Fiach gestured for Shelli, Grian and Jeffrey to sit down.

Grian's seat swung away from him as he climbed awkwardly into it.

"Now," Fiach said when they'd all settled. "Tell me exactly what you're doing here."

"We need to speak to the Council of Colour, and we were told you can take us to them," Grian blurted out nervously.

"Who told you I could take you to them?" Fiach looked anxious now.

"Mother did!" Shelli answered.

"Well, Mother was wrong!" Fiach shook his head before quickly standing up from his seat. "Why would she do that – doesn't she know she's bringing trouble on us! I told Amergin I want no part in this…"

He seemed torn as he shook his head and ran his hands

through his thick hair. Then he looked at the children one more time before leaving the hut and closing the door behind him. Grian heard a faint click and raced over to check the handle.

"He's locked us in!" he gasped, his heart pounding.

CHAPTER 11
THE HSWARM

"He locked us in! Why would he lock us in? Mother said the Wilde would help us!" Grian turned angrily towards Shelli.

"Hey, don't look at me like that," she growled back. "I don't understand either, and de Wilde are our friends. Mother wouldn't have sent us here if they weren't."

"Well, maybe Mother got it wrong…" Grian snapped, pulling at the door handle as his anger slipped into panic.

"She never gets anything wrong!" Shelli jumped off her seat and glared at Grian, her face now crimson red.

"Clearly everyone is rather upset," Jeffrey stated, holding up his hands in peace. "But bickering will not solve this pickle we find ourselves in."

Shelli stamped her foot in frustration before turning away from Grian. She closed her eyes and took a few deep breaths.

"I can't tune in to Mother," she sighed a few minutes later.

Suddenly the handle clicked open and Grian stepped back as an old man with hunched shoulders walked inside the hut, aided by a bramble walking stick. He closed the door behind him before addressing the children.

"I'm Amergin," he whispered urgently. "You're not safe here. You need to go."

"You're de Seer," Shelli whispered. "Mother told you we were coming. She said Fiach would help us!"

"He is helping you – so am I – trust me... De police are watching us and they saw you three enter de forest. They know you are Wilde, Shelli, and so all de Wilde tribes are now being monitored closely. Fiach has to be seen to play his part in order to protect de community. So he's down below with de police now..."

"He's what!?" Grian panicked.

"Trust us. He's playing a game to give you time," Amergin said calmly. "Now take these and go..."

The old man handed him a small brown sack and a stick that looked a little like a wonky Y.

"There's food in de bag and de dowsing stick will help you find your way," Amergin continued.

"Our way where? Where do we go?" Grian stuttered, trying to process what was happening as Amergin herded them towards the door.

"To de desert. Some of de Council are hiding out there in a small town called Dunstan."

"But surely we'll perish crossing the desert!" Jeffrey protested, as they were shepherded out.

"Look for water. Where there's water there's life," Amergin answered mysteriously. Then he placed his finger to his lips to quieten them before leading the three friends quickly across the huge platform, back towards the gates hidden in the wall.

As they walked, Grian could hear loud voices coming from the forest below their feet.

"Let us up to your tree town," someone barked. "The people these children work for are highly dangerous. They destroyed the Tipping Point! Fiach, you are currently obstructing the course of justice!"

"I am obstructing nothing," Fiach replied, sounding fierce. "There is no way for yous to get up to our town, unless ya want to try our trampolines! I have someone bringing them down to us now."

"Is that what you're doing? Are ya bringing us to de police, Amergin?" Shelli growled, as they stopped by the wall where they'd entered.

Her eyes were wild with anger. Amergin planted his

stick on the platform and reached for Shelli. She winced as he placed the tips of his fingers on her forehead.

"I sense you have de Seer's touch, so why don't ya take a look at my soul."

Shelli's eyes closed and her face contorted as if in pain. Grian twitched nervously watching his friend's obvious discomfort, as the voices grew louder in the forest below.

Then Shelli gave a slight whimper before jumping back from Amergin's hand. Her eyes were glassy when she opened them.

"Are you okay?" Grian whispered.

"Yes." She nodded firmly before grabbing the bag of food and the Y stick from Grian's hand and stuffing them into her rucksack. "These people are our friends, they're protecting us. But we need to go. Now."

Amergin rapped the platform with his walking stick and the sentries opened the large nest-like entrance gates.

"Yous need to jump," he whispered. "There's a net hidden under that moss circle below – it's safe."

Grian's legs wobbled as he peered over the edge and spotted a large circle of moss camouflaged so perfectly into the undergrowth that he hadn't noticed it when they'd been down there earlier.

"There's little time. You must go!" Amergin anxiously pushed them towards the edge using his walking stick. "There's much yous three have to do if we're to save this planet. Your young shoulders carry a heavy weight, though I sense it won't break ya. We'll hold de police back as long as we can."

"Thank you." Shelli nodded at the old man before springing from the platform without another word.

Grian trembled as he watched her free-fall. She landed soundlessly on the large, concealed net in the ground and climbed off before gesturing up at him to follow.

His stomach churned. He hesitated, stepping back.

"Go. Now!" Amergin prodded him forward with his stick. "And do not make a sound."

Grian peered over the platform. His heart thumped loudly as he eyed the circle of moss below. It seemed so far away, could he really do it? Amergin prodded him in the back again and Grian wobbled forward. The tips of his shoes were at the edge now. A shiver raced through him almost stealing his breath as he closed his eyes, told his mind to shut up and jumped.

Seconds later he flew through the moss sheet and hit the thick netting only to be bounced back out awkwardly onto the forest floor. He smacked off a protruding root and groaned as fell forward on to his knees. Winded for a moment, he sucked in air.

Then an electric energy coursed through his body. He wanted to scream out in relief and exhilaration but he couldn't, the police were somewhere nearby.

He was just standing up when Jeffrey hurtled through the air into the pit and bounced straight back out, almost knocking Grian off his newly found feet.

Then the nest wall closed, blocking out any light and the forest floor grew suddenly dark. The Wilde town disappeared into the thick jumble of branches above like it had never even existed.

"Come on, quickly!" Shelli hissed, racing off through the trees just as the shouting grew to a crescendo and chaos seemed to break out somewhere in the dense forest behind them.

The Forest of Coll grew on one side of a steep mountain. Grian's legs ached and his lungs heaved.

They'd been running for a while without a word when Jeffrey stopped and almost keeled over. Sweat ran like rivers down his bright red cheeks.

"I'm...I'm...not sure how...how much...longer I can...keep this up!" he wheezed, bending forward at the waist.

Shelli stopped and looked behind them, searching for movement in the trees.

"There is no choice, Jeffrey. We have to keep going. De police are after us," she replied. She wasn't even panting.

"But...but I...I need a break too," Grian admitted, plonking down on a rock nearby while sucking in air.

Shelli rolled her eyes, sighed and threw her rucksack

over at the pair. "Right, maybe some food will hurry ye up."

Grian ignored her obvious frustration, and opened the bag. He shared out a bunch of large juicy grapes and three oranges from the food Amergin had given them. He peeled his orange carefully, pulling off each juicy segment and savouring it in his mouth for a moment before swallowing. He'd never tasted anything so delicious in his whole life, though he'd never been so hungry either.

"I think we may have evaded them," Jeffrey slobbered, swallowing a huge slice of his own orange. His lips dripped in juice.

Grian was about to agree when a small black object landed on the bark of a tree beside him. At first glance it appeared to be a very large fly, but then he watched as the thing morphed into a beetle and scuttled down the trunk to the ground.

His almost choked on his latest orange slice.

"It's a...it's a...an hSwarm!" he stuttered.

"What?" Jeffrey raced over from his spot and watched the hSwarm travel across the undergrowth before disappearing beneath a pile of fallen leaves. "The police must be using the hSwarms too – Hansom must have given them access to all his latest technologies!"

Shelli raced over and grabbed her rucksack, shoving their stuff roughly back inside. Then they all moved behind the cover of a large tree as the hSwarm rustled out of the undergrowth before opening its tiny black metal wings and flying away.

"There might be more of them," Grian whispered, watching the hSwarm disappear into the trees.

"We need to keep moving and keep out of sight," Shelli said. "Come on. Let's go!"

CHAPTER 12

DUNSTAN

Quietly and with more caution the three friends continued up through the forest, watching for any signs of movement. Grian had just entered a small clearing when he spotted a tiny flying beetle above him and ducked back behind a tree.

"There's another one," he hissed, pointing ahead.

They walked round the clearing and continued their climb up the steep forested slope. Grian was jumpy, watching every strange movement around them for signs of the tiny black machines. The things terrified him.

By the time they'd reached the top of the mountain and the end of the forest, his legs ached, his lungs heaved and his head hurt from concentration.

Then Shelli, who was a few steps in front, stopped suddenly and ducked down.

"What is it?" Grian whispered nervously, ducking down too before crawling over to her.

"Look. At de edge of de forest," she pointed.

Grian squinted. Something thick and black clouded the sky just beyond the treeline.

"If I'm not mistaken – and I do have twenty-twenty vision so I very much doubt I am – there appear to be thousands of hSwarms in the sky outside the forest!" Jeffrey stated.

"But we need to get to that place, Dunstan, in the desert! How do we leave the forest? It's impossible – we'll be seen..." Grian felt sick watching the hundreds and thousands of tiny spy machines move through the sky.

"There is no such thing as impossible," Jeffrey scolded him, looking very serious. "Problems can always be solved."

"I think I have an idea," Shelli said quickly. "De last few years it's been raining more than usual in Hopper. I heard Mother and de Aunties talking about it. De weird weather means there are massive swarms of—"

"Not more swarms!" Grian grimaced.

Shelli closed her eyes and descended into a sleep-like state. She sat completely motionless on the mountainside. Grian had seen this before, many times now, and his skin

106

tingled, waiting for something unusual to happen.

After a few minutes the air was filled with the sound of rain. It wasn't raining though. Grian looked around, confused, and held out his hand, but no water wet his palm. Even so, the phantom rains grew stronger until it sounded like they were in the middle of a torrential downpour.

"I'm not talking about Hansom's swarms, Grian," Shelli said loudly, opening her eyes again. "This is a real swarm – a swarm of locusts!"

Shelli stood up and raced to the edge of the forest. Grian and Jeffrey were right behind her. All three stayed just inside the cover of the trees and watched an enormous fast-moving cloud – which appeared to be as wide as the vast desert – soar towards them underneath Hansom's hSwarms. Moments later, the air was heavy with millions upon millions of tiny insects. The insects were pink in colour and so huge in number they blocked out Hansom's tiny spies.

"They've promised to be our cover until we find de Council!" Shelli laughed, raising her hands above her head and racing forward into the living cloud of locusts, before spinning round and round in excitement like a child in a snowstorm. "No one will find us under here. And de locusts have promised not to eat Fiach's food – this plague is here just to save us!"

As she spun, the insects moved with her, forming a tunnel around her body which followed Shelli like a shield wherever she went.

Grian closed his eyes and took a deep breath before stepping into the cloud of flying insects. He was sure they'd swarm all over him and he'd be swatting them away. But when he opened his eyes he discovered that the shield-like tunnel the insects formed around Shelli extended to fit him and then Jeffrey. The three friends walked through the swarm, almost like they were in their own little bubble.

Grian was mesmerized by the millions of pink insects that flapped their wings so rapidly he could barely see them move.

These tiny creatures had chosen to protect him and his friends.

"Thank you!" he cried, throwing his arms up too and spinning round and round in a sudden wave of laughter and gratitude.

"What did you say?" Jeffrey called across to him.

"I wasn't talking to you," he cried back. "I was talking to the locusts!"

Jeffrey said something in return, but Grian couldn't hear him. It was hard to hear above the sound of beating wings.

A sudden lightness fell over him. As he spun in the sea

of pink locusts, Grian felt a part of everything – as if he was one of the insects, or a breeze on the wind or a particle among the trillions of particles of golden desert sand that slid beneath him.

"You are a part of it all – we all are. Now come on, let's find Dunstan," Shelli shouted across to him, before running off.

They'd been running for a while at full steam when Shelli stopped and her feet sank into the now ankle-deep sand.

"I can't see anything clearly ahead," she said as Grian and Jeffrey caught up to her. "We don't know where Dunstan is. I'm afraid we might be going round in circles."

"Amergin told us to use this, that it will help us find the way, remember?" Grian said, pulling the Y-shaped stick from Shelli's rucksack.

"It's just a dowsing stick, Grian," Jeffrey shouted above the beat of a trillion wings. "It's from an era of foolish old wives' tales and it is certainly not a functional method for finding water. If you want my honest opinion, I would imagine it's quite useless really."

"Sometimes we don't want your honest opinion, poshy," Shelli replied, grabbing the stick from Grian.

"So that finds water?" Grian asked excitedly. "Didn't Amergin say 'Where there's water, there's life'! I bet he was giving us a clue. People in towns need water – I'd say if we find water, it'll lead us to Dunstan."

"Amergin isn't a fool," Shelli replied. "I've seen Mother use one of these before."

She held one side of the V end of the stick in each hand and pointed the long part away towards the desert floor, before walking forward. Grian and Jeffrey followed behind, watching closely.

"I can't do this with you two breathing down my neck," Shelli growled over her shoulder.

Grian held back a bit and tried not to worry that they were lost in the desert and instead of the latest Hansom watch with its to-the-millimetre navigational abilities, they were following a stick.

They'd been walking for a while when Shelli gave out a short yelp and jumped in the air.

"I think the straight long bit moves when it's near water," she said excitedly. "And it just moved."

Grian looked around, confused. "But there's no water here."

"I happened to watch a documentary once on subterranean rivers," Jeffrey piped up, wiping sweat from his forehead. "Perhaps we've found an underground river. If we follow it, then it may in fact lead us to Dunstan! Like Amergin said – where there's water there's life!"

"So now you believe in foolish old wives' tales," Shelli replied, raising an eyebrow.

"You're right, Shelli – perhaps old wives' tales aren't all to be dismissed. I imagine we'll find out shortly."

Shelli adjusted their direction whenever the stick twitched and they followed it for what felt like an age through the dry desert. As time wore on, Grian grew more and more exhausted. His legs ached from dragging them through the deep sand, his eyes stung from salt and the soles of his feet felt like they were blistered all over. He was just dreaming of his own bed when a series of shadows emerged like a mirage in the distance.

His heart thumped and his tired body came alive again. Maybe they'd finally find the Council and get some rest and food and answers. Somehow he found the energy to race forward towards the shapes until he was face to face with an enormous worn and weather-beaten sign.

The sign's huge individual letters were cut from corrugated iron and attached to a frame of solid black metal bars. To Grian's relief, the letters spelled DUNSTAN, though roughly spray-painted across the top of the large D, was another word: Dumpstan.

CHAPTER 13

THE SHAFT

"We're here!" Grian whooped. "Dunstan. It's where Amergin told us to go!"

"But there doesn't appear to be anything other than that sign here," Jeffrey said, looking doubtfully around.

Jeffrey was right. Apart from the sign, they were just surrounded by sand. Lots of sand.

"Dunstan..." Jeffrey pondered, over the constant drum of insect wings. "You know, now that I think about it, I've seen a picture of that sign before. Perhaps in geography class? Could Dunstan be a mining town?"

"But if it's a town, where are all de houses?" Shelli asked, squinting through the pink haze of insects.

"Yes, I remember now. That's it exactly, Shelli.

Dunstan is famous because a large percentage of its properties are situated underground, to avoid the desert heat. Which, when you think about it, would make the town a very effective hiding place for the Council of Colour," Jeffrey replied, looking pleased.

"Well, let's go find them then," Grian said, itching to hand the White Rose's letter over to Yarrow.

"We'd better make it a bit easier to search," Shelli said.

She closed her eyes for a moment and suddenly the air cleared. Grian could see round him in all directions. The locusts appeared to have gone, but oddly the rain sound they made hadn't. Grian looked around, confused. Shelli pointed to the sky, and Grian, glancing upwards, startled. A huge flat cloud of locusts blanketed the air, hovering just metres above his head.

"We'll be able to find de Council easier this way, but de locusts' blanket cover is not as good at hiding us as it was when we were surrounded by them. If de hSwarms break through it, they'll see us," Shelli warned. "So be fast and careful."

Grian nodded, and quickly began looking for anything obvious that might help lead the way to the Council.

He spotted a worn dirt track that wound up a slight hill near him and followed it. Shelli and Jeffrey were just behind him.

As he climbed, Grian noticed the steep incline was dotted with lots of holes. Most of the holes were about the size of a saucer, though some were much larger and were probably the diameter of a large bucket. On inspection the holes appeared to be dug deeply into the side of the hill, and each of them, except for the larger ones, was covered in a bubble-like, transparent plastic, like lots of small windows or portholes, making the hill look a little like some sort of weird spaceship.

At the top, Grian could see lots of similar spaceship-like hills dotted through the flat desert landscape nearby. There were also a few clusters of rusty ramshackle huts that looked more like old garden sheds than homes. And there was a tarmac road, half hidden under a wash of sand.

"Do you think de locals live in those huts?" Shelli asked, pointing across to one of the ramshackle buildings.

"Actually I'm quite sure not many people live here at all any more," Jeffrey said, heading down the other side of the hill towards the sandy tarmac road. "From recollection, the mining in Dunstan stopped a number of years ago."

Grian left his friends by the road and headed down to the half concealed tarmac road.

In the distance ahead, he spotted a tall triangular structure made of thin steel beams reaching up from behind another small hill. The structure was so tall the top of it disappeared through the blanket of locusts.

When he was younger, Grian had been addicted to a computer game called "Goldrush" and he played it constantly on his Hansom. The town in the game was full of mineshafts that looked exactly like the A-frame structure he was now staring at.

"I'm going over there," he shouted at the others.

On his climb up the next dusty hill, he passed a burned-out car and a broken sign for an underground motel before reaching the summit.

Quickly he ducked down. The place looked a lot busier from this angle. It seemed like Jeffrey was wrong, the mining hadn't stopped in Dunstan.

A distance below him, under the cloud of locusts, people in hard hats and dirty orange overalls were coming out of the mine through two elevator cages in the centre of the A-framed shaft. Grian watched as they got straight into jeeps parked nearby and drove off in a haze of dust until soon it appeared everyone was gone.

Grian looked back over his shoulder but couldn't see his friends. He didn't want to call them just in case, so he set off to inspect the mine alone.

Stuck at regular intervals along a mesh metal fence that traced the boundary of the mineshaft were large red KEEP OUT and DANGER signs. Grian ignored their warnings as he walked the perimeter until he found a hole in the big enough to climb through.

He looked around quickly before racing across towards the shaft. A set of metal steps ran up the side of the A-framed structure to metal cage elevators above.

Something shimmering on the floor of the first elevator caught Grian's eye. Curious, he climbed the steps up to the lift, wobbling as he stopped short at the door. The elevator was suspended high above a huge black abyss that he could clearly see through the mesh metal floor.

Glistening in the daylight at the far corner of the lift was a small piece of yellow rock crystal. It looked like Shelli's Glimmer or the crystal the White Rose had given Grandad! He held his breath and inched inside the elevator. His hand shook as reached across for the crystal, desperately trying not to look down.

Suddenly Shelli called his name. He wobbled and stumbled backwards, pressing against a small control panel. Out of nowhere a series of loud clanks and clatters filled the air and an orange light began twirling somewhere above his head. Then the lift moved downwards and Grian fell to the floor terrified as it plunged into the abyss.

"Shelli!" he cried.

"Grian! Where are you?" she called from somewhere above.

"I'm in the lift, going into the mine. Help!" he shouted. The blackness that swallowed him was unlike any dark he'd ever experienced. Grian couldn't even see his hand, which he waved in front of his face.

The air chilled rapidly and he started to shiver.

Is this what it'd be like if the sun went out? He closed his eyes and breathed deep, trying to steady his racing heart as the lift chugged further and further into the earth before it clanked to an abrupt stop.

He opened his eyes, but the darkness was so thick that he had to blink to make sure they weren't still closed.

"You! Causing trouble again!" a voice broke through the black.

Then the lift shook a little as someone stepped inside. Frightened, Grian scrambled backward against one of its cold metal sides. Unable to see anything, he had no idea how to escape.

"Grian, Grian! What's happening? Are you okay?" Shelli's panicked voice reached him, sounding tiny this far underground.

He tried to shout back but all that came out was a whimper. His voice was frozen too.

Suddenly a light shone in his eyes. He cowered, blinded, as the rays stabbed his pupils.

"I should give you up to the police myself. It might allow the rest of us to get on with the job in hand. You know the whole of Babbage is looking for you right now, after that stunt you pulled in the Tipping Point. I'd do it, you know, I'd give you up – if the police weren't looking for me too!"

As his eyes adjusted, Grian could just make out a face. "Vermilion!" he gasped.

CHAPTER 14

DAD

"How...? What..." Grian stuttered, taken aback.

The last time he'd seen Vermilion, Grian had knocked him out in the Tipping Point using hThoughtTech gloves.

Vermilion was a member of the Council of Colour and had been working undercover in Howard Hansom's organization in the Tipping Point, in order to find out what Hansom was up to – until Grian, Jeffrey and Shelli had accidently blown his cover. Grian had a feeling Vermilion hadn't forgiven them for that.

Vermilion wasn't one of Grian's favourite people either though, since he'd tried to stop Grian and his grandad saving Shelli from Hansom. He remembered the callous look in the tall man's eyes when he told them to think of the bigger picture. His words were something like, "Do you want to save that girl or save our sun?" That was just before Grian knocked him out.

"You're lucky I set a camera on the mineshaft. Be more careful," Vermilion barked, pointing his torch accusingly. "You messed things up for me once. I warn you, don't try it again! Now what are you doing here? I imagine this is not a coincidence!"

"I, ahem…we…" Grian stuttered in shock, still unable to find his voice.

"What's going on here?" A woman appeared in the shadows behind Vermilion.

In the spill of light, Grian could see she had dark golden skin and was wearing a long yellow dress that fell loosely over a pair of yellow trousers.

"This is Adler's grandson," Vermilion said over his shoulder. "You should recognize him, he's famous now. Or maybe infamous is a better word!"

"Grian, where are you? We're coming down!" Shelli called, as the distant sound of the second lift cranked and rattled somewhere in the darkness above.

"Great! Why not just alert all Dunstan to the fact that you're here!" Vermilion snapped, looking a little panicked as he glared upwards. "And give away my hiding spot – it's not like you haven't done it before!"

"Who are they, these people who are coming for you?"

the woman asked Grian. Her voice was calm though she sounded concerned.

"My friends," he replied nervously.

The woman narrowed her dark eyes. "What are you and your friends doing in Dunstan?"

Grian wasn't sure what to say, until his gaze fell across a small round pin on the breast pocket of the woman's dress. It was a colour wheel: the symbol of the Council.

"We're, ahem...we're looking for the Council of Colour," he said.

Though the air had a distinct chill this deep underground, Grian broke out in a sweat.

"And what do you know of the Council?" the woman asked, still looking suspicious as the lift carrying Shelli and Jeffrey came to a halt beside them.

"What's he doing here?!" Shelli growled, grabbing the lift bars as she spotted Vermilion.

"The miners have finished up for the day but there may still be some about – let's not do this here. Come with me!" the woman said, turning quickly on her heels.

Grian, Jeffrey and Shelli stumbled out of the cage-like lifts and watched her switch on her own hand torch before leading them swiftly along a corridor of rough-cut rock supported by intervals of thick red steel.

"Keep up," Vermilion snarled, poking Grian in the back.

Grian shuffled forward faster. He was behind the

woman when she turned in through a heavy metal door. On the other side, a concrete stairwell greeted them.

"The mine is deeper than the town. These stairs lead up to the subterranean streets," she said taking the first step.

Dripping water echoed through the space giving Grian the shivers.

"Who is that lady?" Jeffrey whispered.

"I don't know, but she's wearing a Council pin. She must be a member," Grian replied, desperately hoping he was right.

They reached the top of the stairs and the woman stopped at another heavy metal door. She turned round and looked at all three children.

"Most people have up and left Dunstan, so it's not a busy town. But even still, keep your heads down," she ordered. "Do not make eye contact with anyone. You are wanted by the authorities – remember that."

She opened the door and quickly ushered Grian, Jeffrey and Shelli out onto what appeared to be an underground street. Small black metal lanterns gently lit the tunnel-like space. They were hanging from hooks screwed into a rock ceiling.

The woman led them quickly past boarded-up shops cut deep into the rock on either side of the street. The shops had names like Desert Desserts and Gem Jewellers hanging from faded signs over their closed front doors. Grian lowered his head when a man walked by and ducked into Bob's Bookies, which, along with The Dunstan Dingo Bingo Palace, appeared to be the only places still in use.

Then the woman stopped outside a paint-chipped, red door and turned the key. She stepped back and directed them inside the cave-like home where family pictures hung in dusty frames along a small dark entrance hall.

The floor in the kitchen was covered in orange red tiles and the walls were whitewashed and rough. A row of white kitchen units and a buzzing white fridge lined one wall and in the middle of the room was a small round table hidden under a flower-patterned cloth. Past the table, behind a low wall that divided the space, the kitchen stepped down into a sunken sitting room with a shabby white couch.

As they walked in, a man stood up from his seat on the couch.

"Grian!" the man uttered, paling in shock.

His face looked dry and cracked like the desert floor, and his lips were covered in blistering sores. His eyes were bloodshot and his hair was chalked in white sand, but Grian knew him straight away.

"Dad!" he cried, racing down the step and into his father's open arms.

CHAPTER 15

YARROW

"What are you doing here, Grian?" his dad asked, after they'd hugged for what felt like an age. "Your mother went to find you in the Wilde forest. She must be worried sick."

Grian blushed and looked away. He itched to tell his dad about the letter he carried, but he couldn't, he had to find Yarrow.

"Solas knows I'm here, she said she'd tell Mam, so Mam won't worry," Grian replied quickly. "I, ahem...we came to—"

"We came to find ya, sir," Shelli interrupted. "In case ya needed our help!"

124

"Yeah…yeah, in case you need our help," Grian added, grasping on to Shelli's made-up explanation.

"I've only really arrived here myself – how did you know where I'd be?" his dad asked, confused. "I was at the Postal meeting when I got word Grandad was missing and you were in the Wilde forest. When your mam came to meet me, we decided she'd go to the forest to get you. I don't understand what's going on. And who are your two friends?"

"Haven't you seen the news, Dad?" Grian asked.

"No. I've been trying to get here…"

"What about your Hansom? Are you wearing it?" Grian panicked, lifting up his father's wrist and pulling back his sleeve.

"No, Grian, I left it behind. That's why I got lost so many times. I'm here on a special visit for…work. I, ahem…" His father faltered, clearly trying his best to hide the truth too. They were both keeping secrets.

"You're here because you have a letter from the White Rose," Grian blurted out. "We know, Dad."

His father's mouth dropped open a little and he shook his head before Grian launched into the story of their adventures over the past few days and how he had become the most hated boy in Babbage.

"But I don't…I don't… How could Hansom do that – you're just children!"

"And not very clever ones at that," Vermilion, sitting at the kitchen table, snarled under his breath.

Grian's dad glared over at the man.

"Right, it's late," the woman in yellow said. "You three look exhausted, and by the sounds of it you've had a very busy day. You need some sleep! If you're as infamous as Vermilion says then you will need your wits about you to stay out of trouble."

Grian didn't argue. Even though his stomach grumbled, and he was dying to catch up with his dad, his body felt as if it longed for sleep above all else.

"I would quite like the opportunity to eat something first," Jeffrey announced, opening the fridge to peer inside.

"For once I agree with ya, poshy," Shelli said, looking a little relieved.

"Oh of course, I wasn't thinking." The woman laughed, pulling some bread from a drawer. "It's difficult to sleep on an empty stomach."

Once they'd all had a quick sandwich, the woman led the children across the sitting room, into a narrow corridor on the other side. Four doors led off the corridor.

One of the doors was ajar, and as they passed it, Grian spotted some two-way radio equipment on a table in the room. The equipment looked like a pared-down version of his grandad's set-up that rested under the stairs in Grian's house.

"Here's your room," the woman said, pushing open the last door.

The room inside was small. A set of bunk beds with hot-air-balloon patterned duvet covers looked squashed in the tight space. The rough white walls were decorated in a cloud-like pattern giving it the air of a child's bedroom.

"These homes have all been empty a while now," the woman explained, her tone gentle. "I think life in Dunstan was hard. So once they got the opportunity, a lot of the miners and their families moved to the Tipping Point..."

Grian shuddered. The names Andy and Grace were painted cheerfully onto the wooden headboards of each bunk. His mind was pulled suddenly back to the thousands of happy, smiling people talking enthusiastically about their new move to the Tipping Point on the screen walls of the Hyperloop platform. Were Andy and Grace on those walls?

He tried to block out the memory of empty warehouse cages underneath the smart city. What had happened to all those people who'd volunteered to save the world?

"I'm afraid you'll have to share the beds, but there should be enough room. And there's blankets in the wardrobe if you need them." The woman nodded, pulling Grian from his memories.

Grian coughed. "Ahem…" He needed to say this without Vermilion around – he didn't know yet if they could trust him.

"Yes," she said. "What is it?"

"We have to find Yarrow, the head of the Council of Colour. There's something I have to give them." There was immediate relief as the words tumbled out.

"And what might that be?" the woman asked, raising her eyebrows.

"I can't…I can't say. The message is only for Yarrow," he finished, blushing.

"You know, yarrow is a resilient yellow flower," the woman stated.

Grian's blush grew deeper as he shook his head, confused.

"My understanding, though I am not a botanical expert," Jeffrey said, holding a blanket he'd just taken from the wardrobe, "is that yarrow is not always yellow."

"You are right, though yellow is my favourite variety of the flower."

"So you are Yarrow. Is that what ya're telling us?" Shelli asked.

"Yes." The woman smiled gently, sitting down on a small child's stool shaped like an elephant. "That's my Council name. Now, what is it you have to tell me?"

Grian looked at his friends. When they'd both nodded

in silent understanding he took out the plastic bag from his pocket and removed the small cream hessian pouch from inside. To his relief the plastic had done its job and the pouch wasn't wet.

"Then this is for you!" His hand trembled passing over the bag.

Grian felt able to breathe for the first time since he'd watched his grandad leave on the Hyperloop with Howard Hansom. He'd done what Grandad had asked him to do and he'd kept it a secret. Well, almost a secret. An unexpected tear rolled down his cheek. He wiped it away, hoping no one had noticed.

Yarrow stared at the small bag in her hand.

"It's from the White Rose," Grian almost whispered.

"Did the White Rose give it to you?" Yarrow asked surprised.

"No," Grian shook his head, "my grandad – Adler – did. He said I was only to give it to you, and that I had to keep it a secret."

"But it's clearly not a secret..." Yarrow glanced at Shelli and Jeffrey.

Grian looked at the floor, his cheeks growing even redder.

"Carrying something like this can't have been easy, especially on young shoulders," Yarrow continued. "I understand why you told your friends."

"We're a team," Shelli answered proudly.

Shelli smiled at Grian as Jeffrey gave a reassuring shrug. His friend was right. They were a team, a really good team.

Yarrow opened the drawstring without a word and turned the bag over. The small piece of yellow rock crystal fell out onto her palm.

"There's a letter too," Grian urged.

Yarrow studied the crystal, watching closely as it shimmered in the light from the small ceiling shaft above their heads.

"It looks like citrine," she whispered. "The sun stone."

Gently she opened the letter. The lines on her face deepened as she read. Her hand moved unconsciously to her cheek and tears pooled round her eyes. When she finished, she folded the page back up and sighed, holding it to her chest.

"So it is true. There is a way we can stop this madness. And now we have two letters," she half whispered, before addressing Grian. "Did Adler tell you anything about the White Rose? It appears from this letter that he may know who they are?"

"No," he replied. "But Grandad didn't have much time to tell me, even if he'd wanted to…"

Grian explained what had happened that night in the Tipping Point. He tried not to let his voice tremble when he got to the bit where Grandad walked onto the Hyperloop and disappeared with Hansom.

"So you are a piece of this puzzle," Yarrow said, addressing the crystal.

"What did ya call it again – citrus?" Shelli asked.

"Citrine," Yarrow answered. "I'm an astronomer but I've also studied minerology – it helps to understand my field. Citrine is a type of quartz. Ancient cultures would say it's a gift from the sun. It's found commonly in the Quantum district of Babbage, there are huge caves of it there, but there are some deposits here in Dunstan too."

"That must be why I saw a chunk of it in the lift earlier," Grian said, thinking out loud.

"I doubt it," Yarrow replied. "They don't mine for it here – citrine isn't valuable. They mine opal in Dunstan. It fetches a much higher price with jewellers."

"Oh," Grian answered confused. He was sure it was the same stone he'd left behind in the lift.

"Did ancient people think citrine was a gift from de sun because of de way it lights up?" Shelli asked.

"I don't know what you mean." Yarrow frowned.

Shelli took her Glimmer from her bag, and closed her eyes. After a few seconds the rock began to slowly pulse light round the room.

Yarrow gasped. "What – how... Where did you get that?"

"It's my Glimmer – Mother gave it to me," Shelli answered. "It has to be de same type of crystal as de one that came with that letter. Watch."

Shelli took the White Rose's smaller crystal from Yarrow's hand and closed her eyes again. It too began to pulse with light.

"How did you do that?" Yarrow shook her head, astonished.

"I just thought of Mam," Shelli answered, before handing back the smaller stone. "The crystals light when you think of someone ya love."

Yarrow looked sceptical. She took back the crystal and cupped her hand around the small object, waiting a moment before closing her eyes too. Slowly the crystal began to light again.

"Wow." She gulped in awe. "I've never seen anything like that before! I know people use crystals for all kinds of pseudo-science. There have been some real scientific studies into them too, though: the Curie brothers discovered if we change their temperature and put pressure on them, crystals can conduct electricity. Perhaps this is something to do with that...though the pressure I am putting on it in my palm is very light and the temperature change minimal. I'd like to look at this crystal's composition. It might give us an idea as to why or how it lights. That might help us understand why it plays a part in the larger puzzle the White Rose writes about."

"And you won't tell Vermilion about the letter?" Grian blurted out, before wishing he hadn't.

Yarrow furrowed her brow. "You can trust Vermilion. He has a hard edge, but he is on our side."

Grian nodded, blushing a little again as Yarrow got up and put the package his grandad had given him into her pocket.

"Now you three get some sleep. We have much to do tomorrow," she said before leaving the room.

"I really hope she doesn't tell Vermilion about Grandad's letter," Grian said, changing out of his clothes into a dinosaur T-shirt the family must have left behind, before climbing onto the bottom bunk. "I know he's a Council member but there's just something about him..."

Exhausted, Grian felt like he'd turned to liquid and seeped right into the mattress. His heavy eyes began to close, and his only discomfort now was the slight ache of his blistered feet throbbing a little beneath the duvet.

"Well, it's in Yarrow's hands now – like your granda wanted," Shelli said, curling up on the floor, insisting it was more comfortable than the beds.

"Two letters found, if we include your grandad's secret letter, and two still to find," Jeffrey mumbled, scaling the ladder to the top bunk. "The odds are beginning to move a little in our favour."

The door creaked and Grian startled from his slumber as a shadow moved quickly away down the corridor. Had somebody been listening to them outside or was he being paranoid?

He liked Yarrow. She seemed, as Jeffrey once said, like "the good type of adult", but Vermilion – Grian wasn't sure he trusted him yet. It was the last thought he had before he closed his eyes and sleep came thick and fast.

CHAPTER 16

THE LIBRARY

Sore and stiff, Grian climbed slowly out of bed the following morning. Shelli was already up and dressed, and was flicking through a book as Grian put his clothes on. Jeffrey was the last to rise, yawning deeply as he got ready.

When they reached the kitchen, Vermilion and his dad were huddled over a piece of paper.

"Is that the letter you found, Dad?" Grian asked, rushing to his side as Shelli and Jeffrey followed behind.

Vermilion held up his hand to stop them.

"Before you consider reading it aloud, Cam," he glared at the children, "have you three got any technology on your person at all?"

Grian, Jeffrey and Shelli shook their heads.

"No Hansom watches or hTablets?" he continued.

"We said we don't, didn't we," Shelli growled, her top lip curling upwards.

Vermilion seemed to be one of those adults who never believed what kids told him. Grian didn't like that type of grown-up. A teacher in his school was like that; she even gave a boy detention once for lying about not doing his homework because his great-granny died, and only let him off when his parents came in with a certificate to prove she had.

"Right. Go ahead then, Cam," Vermilion finally said, turning back to the table.

His dad grimaced and Grian could tell from the look on his face that he wasn't sure what to make of Vermilion either. Then he cleared his throat and began to read. His hands were shaking a little as he held the page.

"Dear Postman,
Only the Poet can see,
What's truly reflected in me,
I'm precious to the night sky,
Of my majesty I am not shy.
For I'm as black as the jaguar sun,
And in my heart the battle is won.
The White Rose."

"Hmm…" Jeffrey sighed, sitting down at the table. "Now that certainly is a puzzle!"

Grian peered over his dad's shoulder, studying the letter. The handwriting was definitely the same as the handwriting in the letter his grandad had given him so they must have been written by the same person. He bit down on his thumbnail, mulling over the rhyme. It was a habit his mam always gave out to him about.

Because Grian's grandad loved puzzles, they had grown up with them in his house. His grandad's favourites were puzzle boxes, but he also loved riddles, wordsearches and crosswords. He'd told Grian they kept his mind young. The White Rose seemed to love puzzles too: in their letter they'd said they played puzzles with Grian's grandad, which meant Grandad must have known them well. So who could the White Rose be?

"Like I told you both already, I really believe the jaguar sun is the place to start breaking this riddle apart," Yarrow said, entering the room. "The phrase rings a bell. I know I've heard of it before, I'm just not sure where."

"If I could get on the hNet, even for a mere moment," Jeffrey whispered, echoing Grian's thoughts, "I'm sure I'd have the puzzle solved remarkably quickly."

"Well, you can't!" Shelli snapped. "We can't risk anyone finding us or de Council."

"But, on a risk-benefit analysis," Jeffrey muttered, "I

137

feel we could afford the risk. It'd be so much quicker, and what is the statistical likelihood of—"

"You know, when I was young we used books to do our research," Grian's dad interrupted, smiling. "And as far as I know they still can't be hacked or tracked."

"Oh yes, encyclopedias were the hNet of my youth," Yarrow agreed.

"How about a library then," Jeffrey said excitedly. "There must be one in Dunstan?"

Yarrow walked over to a kitchen drawer and pulled out a faded tourist leaflet with the sentence *Welcome to Dunstan: Hopper's Little Gem* on the front cover. She opened it flat and flipped over the page to reveal a map.

"Because I haven't been in Dunstan long, this map helps me navigate the place," she said. "Not that I leave the house much."

The map was divided into light and dark brown areas. The light-brown areas showed everything above ground, like the mineshaft and the tourist office. The dark-brown areas highlighted everything underground, like the church, houses, shops, a cinema, some restaurants and...

"There it is – the library!" Jeffrey exclaimed, stabbing the map with his finger.

"That doesn't mean it's open," Yarrow replied, "half the things on this map aren't any more."

"But it's not far from here either," Shelli said. "It looks

to be at the end of de main underground street. We could go check?"

Grian jumped up, itching to get moving. "Let's go then."

"You know I prefer we don't go out, Yarrow. Unless completely necessary," Vermilion said.

"I think I can decide when going out is appropriate, Vermilion," she replied a little sharply.

"But we were out yesterday evening bringing this lot back, and if people become too familiar with seeing us they may ask questions. A group this big would look suspicious. Why take that risk for something that may not be open and probably will not further our cause? No one can get wind that members of the Council are here – especially you, Yarrow. You are indispensable."

"And we are probably not." Shelli smirked at Vermilion. "So that means we can go alone!"

"No. Everyone is looking for you three!" Grian's dad shook his head. "I'm not risking your safety. I'll go. No one is looking for me."

"Maybe Vermilion is right," Yarrow spoke slowly, her words considered, "we should be a bit more cautious right now. And so far nobody is aware that you have anything to do with any of this, Cam, so perhaps it is safest if you go to the library."

"Dunstan is very remote and has all the appearances of

being quite backward, so our notoriety may not have travelled here yet," Jeffrey argued. "I really believe I would be a huge asset to this operation and I'd quite like to spend some time in a library. I'm a rather good researcher, even via old-fashioned methods."

"Jeffrey's right – I bet they don't know us here yet," Grian pleaded looking from his dad to Yarrow. "Please let us go too?"

His father eventually caved in, after continuous rounds of pleading. "Okay, but only if Yarrow agrees?"

"If you three stay quiet and don't draw any unwanted attention then you can go. Dunstan is a sleepy and half deserted town. Three children and their father making a library visit is normal enough not to draw suspicion, I imagine."

"But you three will do whatever I say," Grian's father piped up.

"Of course. I'd have it no other way, Cam!" Jeffrey smiled, slapping Grian's dad on the back.

Grian spurted out the mouthful of water he'd just taken in and tried to hold back his laughter as his father shot Jeffrey one of his Don't-mess-with-me looks.

As added precaution, Yarrow found some hats to disguise them a little. Shelli's was large and floppy and she stuffed her nest of red curls into it, hiding them away. Grian and Jeffrey wore baseball caps with Dunstan Dinos, the local football club, written across the front.

They set off for the library, awkwardly using their paper map as a guide. Sometimes Grian longed for how easy everything was with a Hansom.

They walked past Bob's Bookies, where a handful of people wearing jeans and mullet hairstyles shouted at a TV screen mounted high on the stone wall, and on past more boarded-up shopfronts until they reached the post office, by far the liveliest premises on the street.

"It's a treat to see people still using the post." Grian's father smiled as they stopped briefly outside to look in. "You know, the Dunstan branch is one of our busiest in the country!"

Grian had forgotten how much his dad loved his work. Whenever they went anywhere he had to check out the local post office, always embarrassingly calling in to say hello. "The postal service is one big happy family," he constantly told them.

They continued on for a short while before coming to a stop under another faded sign. This one would have read Dunstan Library except the D in the sign had fallen off, leaving a dirty outline of its shape.

The main window of the library was littered in faded notices for babysitting, housekeeping and missing cats. There were also posters for the Tipping Point, which was weird. Grian had only ever seen it advertised on his

Hansom or the hNet. It was a little reassuring though, like Jeffrey said, Dunstan did appear a little old-fashioned.

"A poster," Jeffrey smirked. "This place is truly antiquated!"

A bell tingled above their heads when they stepped inside the glass front door.

The library seemed to be small. A blue carpet, greyed in part by wear, covered the stone floor, while the rough-cut rock walls and ceiling were whitewashed, just like the home they were staying in. Rows and rows of cream metal bookshelves on wheels divided up the space.

"It really is quite primitive," Jeffrey whispered. "I wonder if they will even have encyclopedias?"

Shelli shushed him, squinting angrily at their friend.

Someone coughed and cleared their throat. The noise rang out in the quiet space.

A small woman wearing thick, brown glasses stood up from behind a desk hidden in the corner of the room. A mop of purple-tinted curly hair surrounded her squat, square face. A rectangle of blue light hovered on her cream blouse from the screen of an old block-like computer resting on the desk in front of her.

"Do I know you?" the librarian accused, in the slow drawl of her Hopper accent. "Or are you guys from outta town? There's just something familiar about you all…"

CHAPTER 17

THE JAGUAR SUN

Cam Woods looked much more relaxed than Grian felt turning to nod at his son.

"Why don't you three go along and pick out some books, while I speak to this nice librarian," he said, smiling through gritted teeth.

"Okay, Pops!" Jeffrey replied cheerily.

Grian held back a nervous snigger. Jeffrey always said weird things when he tried act normal.

"Wow," Jeffrey said, pocketing a small rectangular plastic card which was stuck to a leaflet on a table near the door. "It's to sign up for an actual library card, a physical one – isn't that quaint. I've always wanted one of these. They only use the app in Tallystick."

"Make sure your hands are clean, children! It's not my job to wipe grime off book covers," the librarian piped up, as the threesome headed towards the bookshelves.

The library was tiny compared to the one in Tallystick and was divided up by aisles of cream-coloured metal shelving. The books were stacked mainly spine out and covered in what looked like some kind of shiny plastic.

Unlike here, the library in Tallystick didn't have many physical books; it was filled mostly with podcast studios and game recording labs, and you never had to look for anything yourself. You just told the computer what you wanted and an automatic trolley went and got it or sent your Hansom a download link.

"You must love this place," Grian whispered to Jeffrey while they searched the aisles. "Anytime I was in the library back home, you were there too."

"Father dropped me there regularly when he had somewhere to be, and he had somewhere to be quite a lot. It's a virtual child's playground, he says, and he's not wrong. Worlds are built on stories."

A now familiar pang of guilt hit Grian. He probably should have been friendlier to Jeffrey in the past. After all, they were neighbours.

"When this is all over, you can come to my house whenever your dad has somewhere to be," Grian replied.

"I certainly intend to, thank you, Grian." Jeffrey

smiled at him. "I feel we are great friends now. Friends for life, I dare say! Though we'll have to save the sun if we've any chance of continuing our friendship."

Grian laughed before he could stop himself. Jeffrey did have a way of being funny, even if he didn't know it himself. The other boy shrugged before turning back to the bookshelves.

The shelves were covered in handwritten stuck-on labels in alphabetical order.

"I'm not sure we'll find anything in here," Shelli hissed from the opposite aisle, poking her head through an empty section in the middle shelf to look at Grian. "There's too many books. It'll take years!"

"Just look for the encyclopedic section. I'm sure there must be one somewhere," Jeffrey encouraged.

Behind them, things were getting heated between his dad and the librarian. Grian peered round the shelf to where they were standing. The librarian's face was flushed, and she was wagging her index finger at his dad. Grian tensed: Yarrow warned them not to draw any attention.

"Over here," Shelli said, pulling his thoughts back to their search.

She was standing at the back wall, which was lined in thick navy books. Grian walked closer. *Encyclopedia Babbagica* was written on the side of every spine, in shiny gold letters.

"Great work, Shelli!" Jeffrey clapped, walking towards them.

He reached up and pulled out a very large book. It was numbered 4 and marked H–Kn. Jeffrey struggled under its weight, heaving it onto a nearby reading table.

Shelli and Grian peered over his shoulder as he flicked confidently through the pages.

"Yarrow seems interested in the jaguar sun, so I thought perhaps I'd start with looking up the word jaguar," he said, his nose almost touching the thin white paper while studying the text.

After a few seconds, Jeffrey stabbed the page with his index finger.

"There – jaguar." He nodded at the word in bold font.

Grian shivered, silently reading the text.

The name jaguar comes from the Tupt-Guarani word meaning "He who kills with one leap".

He skimmed through the paragraph until another scary sentence stopped him.

For the past twenty years the species has been threatened, due to human encroachment on their habitat.

"What does 'encroachment' mean?" he asked, without looking up.

"It means we're cutting down de jaguars' home to make room for cities and stuff like digital forests," Shelli replied sourly. "It's like what's happening to that badger family ya saw earlier, Grian, or what happened to Nach. It just means humans are greedy!"

"Well, technically it doesn't mean that, Shelli. You've added quite a lot of emotion to the text." Jeffrey frowned.

"Do you think people are bad?" Grian asked no one in particular. He wasn't even sure he wanted an answer.

"No. Most people are very good in fact, Grian," Jeffrey replied, with his usual certainty. "Most humans want to love and be loved. There are of course some bad people in the world, though studies have consistently shown a vast majority of these people have a lack of love in their own lives."

Grian squirmed at the word "love". Why was Jeffrey always so weird?

"Howard Hansom is bad and he hasn't had a lack of love. De whole world loves him!" Shelli huffed.

Hansom was a bad person – Grian knew Shelli was right about that – but, like Jeffrey, he wanted to believe people were good and that in the end the good people always won.

When the earthquake happened, his mam had told him and Solas to look out for the good people. She said they were the helpers. And at that time there were helpers everywhere.

But how would the good people know to help, if they believed Hansom's stories in the news were true?

147

Everybody, including the police, was so distracted looking for Grian and his friends that they'd forgotten about the sun: it was all working out exactly how Howard Hansom said it would, the night he'd taken Grandad away on the Hyperloop.

Grian closed his eyes. His breath grew rapid, and he felt faint. He steadied himself against the desk. This weird, panicked feeling had happened once before, after the earthquake. At that time, his grandad told him it was because he feared his thoughts. He said to remember thoughts were just stories we told ourselves.

"It'll be okay," Shelli whispered, gripping his shoulder. "We'll save de sun and all de good people."

"But you don't like people. You think all people are bad," Grian snapped, a sudden anger firing inside.

"I don't think all people are bad," Shelli replied. "I just think most adults like to ignore what's happening because life is easier that way; even if so much of de sun is dark now it's impossible to ignore. I think they're scared, but I think it's okay to be scared. When I'm scared I do something so that I'm not scared any more."

Grian wavered. "But I'm scared and I'm doing something, that doesn't mean we'll save the sun though?"

"But you have to believe we will, Grian – that's what Mother says. When you believe something de energy you create trying to make that belief real, joins de energy of all

148

de other people who believe de same thing. That's how what you believe becomes real." Shelli's eyes were more alive than he had ever seen them.

Grian felt a surge of excitement too. Her enthusiasm had somehow rubbed off on him.

He picked up a pencil lying on the desk and started writing down some of the details that stood out about jaguars from the opened page of the encyclopedia. Nothing in the text mentioned the word "sun" though, so he wasn't sure how useful it would be.

"Maybe we're concentrating on the word 'jaguar' when we should be looking at the word 'sun'?" he said, thinking aloud.

He finished his notes and raced back to the bookshelf, pulling out the encyclopedia marked Sp–T.

He flicked through the thick book until he found the word Sun. Then felt a little sick reading the first sentence.

The sun is the source of an enormous amount of energy, a portion of which provides Earth with the light and heat necessary to support life.

He scanned down through the rest of the listings under the word Sun, stopping on phrases like sun river, sun dog, sun orchid, and sun worship. He was scribbling down as much from each of the sections as he could when his dad walked over to join them.

"I think we should get going," his dad whispered,

looking both nervous and hassled.

"But to be effective we really need quite a number of hours here, Mr Woods," Jeffrey complained. "We can't be expected to perform miracles! This is a very old-fashioned and labour-intensive method of research. It takes time."

"We can't spend any longer here," Dad replied, shaking his head. "That woman is very suspicious of us. She asked me lots of questions about where we came from and didn't seem to like the fact that I had no identification on me. I found this in a pile near the door too." He held a rolled-up newspaper in his hand. "I think it's best we go."

"What's in the paper, Dad?" Grian asked, feeling his nerves returned.

"If we're leaving, then we simply must take these with us," Jeffrey interrupted, stumbling under the weight of the two encyclopedias he'd just picked up. "I'm registered on the Babbage library system. I should be able to take these out."

"No," Grian hissed, pulling on Jeffrey's jumper before he walked away.

The librarian stood up behind her desk watching the commotion.

"You can't take those, I'm afraid." She nodded at the books in Jeffrey's arms. "Only members can take books from the library."

"We're not taking them, we're just leaving," Grian's

dad said, grabbing the books from Jeffrey's arms and planting them back on the table.

"There's no need to rush away!" The woman smiled, looking suddenly very friendly. "If that boy would like to be a member I can sign him up. All I need is a name."

Grian and Shelli rushed past the librarian with their heads down, almost squashing each other at the door in their rush to get outside. Jeffrey mumbled a polite apology to the librarian before joining them on the street, his face flushed. He was followed quickly by Grian's dad, who also looked flustered.

All four walked briskly away when the librarian appeared out on the street.

"Where did you say you were staying again?" she called after them.

Grian's dad mumbled something incoherent before turning down a random side alley, in the opposite direction from the way they had come.

CHAPTER 18
THE UNTOLD TRUTH

They took an alternative route back to the home they were staying in. Every time Grian's dad stopped to consult the map, he checked over his shoulder. Grian had never seen him so rattled. Usually, nothing fazed his dad, and the world felt safe – now, nothing felt safe.

When they reached the house they all raced inside and his dad locked the door behind them before heading straight into the kitchen.

"What's happened?" Yarrow asked, concerned, standing up from her place on one of the shabby white couches in the sitting room area.

"The librarian was suspicious, and I found this," his dad replied, unrolling the newspaper he'd been carrying on the table.

Across the top of the paper, in ornate lettering, were the words *The Dunstan Daily*. Under it, in the centre on the front page, was a large black and white photo of a distressed old woman. The woman was wearing oversized sunglasses and her ice-white hair was slicked back in a bun. Slightly blurred in the background of the image was a fire engine and an ambulance, as though she was standing in the middle of an emergency scene.

The headline read:

Adorabelle Hansom visits the Tipping Point to thank emergency crews, who are still looking for her son Howard Hansom, the tech entrepreneur.

"But I don't under—"

"Not there, Grian. There!" Shelli pointed to the bottom of the page where headshots of the three children and Vermilion were lined up under a big red WANTED banner.

"I'm sure the librarian has seen it. She asked a lot of questions. But even if she hasn't, others will have. It's… it's in the local paper!" his dad stammered.

"We need to leave. Soon." Yarrow started pacing the room. "We'll go at first dark, when it's safer."

"You don't need to go, Yarrow." Grian's dad shook his head. "We've brought this danger here. It's Grian and the others the police are looking for. We'll go. You stay."

"No, we'll all go. There's another safe house not too

far from here, in Hopper City. Vermilion is on our two-way radio at the minute, talking to other Council members, so I'll ask him to alert them to the change of plan," Yarrow replied, before she quickly swept from the room.

To distract himself from the nervous activity around him, Grian took out the notes he'd written in the library and began to study them.

"Did ya find anything that might help us understand de White Rose's puzzle?" Shelli quizzed.

"I don't know. See what you think." He shrugged and began to read the random words he'd written down out loud. "Sun, astronomy – star around which the earth revolves. Source of enormous energy. Sun orchid – plant genus of about hundred species of orchid. Sun worship – many ancient cultures such as the Aztecs and Mayas relied heavily on the worship of—"

"That's it!" Yarrow exclaimed, entering the room once more. "The Aztecs! That's where I've heard of the jaguar sun before. I'm certain it has something to do with the Aztecs – a nomadic ancient tribe of people."

She sat down quickly and pulled Grian's notes over towards her, studying them for a minute before handing them back.

"Huh. I just…I remember learning something about it at uni. The Aztecs were skilled astronomers. Their temples even aligned with the sun. I'm sure it will come to me. If only I had my textbooks, but I had to leave everything behind...I can't go home since I spoke out." Yarrow looked a little sad.

"Why did you speak out?" Grian asked, thinking about his grandad and how everyone in Tallystick thought he was mad for speaking his mind about Hansom and the Tilt.

"Because the truth is the most important thing we have. I took to the hNet and told the virtual world how my scientific evidence proved the earth hadn't tilted. After a while my social accounts were suspended, and then someone – I presume Hansom – had a word with my university and I lost my job. But out of all that drama, something beautiful blossomed. Other like-minded people contacted me, and we began to work together.

"Many of us received death threats and went into hiding. I'm constantly on the move. Everyone in the group uses an alias, and as a collective we became the Council of Colour. The name is a symbol of our diversity of opinion and backgrounds. Together we share findings and whether we agree or disagree, everyone gets a fair hearing – that's true science, ever-changing because it's ever-questioned. Only that way we will find out the truth of what's happening and be able to work to fix the sun..."

"How close are you to the truth?" Grian asked.

"We know some things but there's lots we don't know. That's my honest answer," Yarrow replied.

Then she got up and left the room, before returning with rolls of paper. She unrolled the large sheets to reveal drawings of what looked to be the earth and the sun surrounded by complicated equations.

"The sun sends energy to the earth," Yarrow began to explain. "Some of that energy is lost to the atmosphere, some is reflected or absorbed by the clouds and some is absorbed into the earth. This exchange of energy is vital to our survival here on this planet and it has been constant since records began. That is, except for two days in recent history…"

"What two days?" Jeffrey asked wide-eyed.

"The day of the earthquake and the day of the Tipping Point explosion. On both those days, the energy the earth received from the sun was not reflected or absorbed by the atmosphere. Something unusual and unprecedented happened – it simply disappeared! And on the first of those days the black mark appeared, and on the second it grew."

"The sun's energy just disappeared!? How?" Shelli asked, almost climbing out of her seat.

"We're not sure how," Yarrow answered. "We know the sun's energy disappeared in a specific spot when it reached our atmosphere. There is nothing like this phenomenon recorded in history, and we can't find an energy loss like this replicated anywhere in nature, so... we think it's man-made."

"Man-made!" Grian's dad looked shocked.

"The sun *is* being stolen," Grian whispered suddenly remembering a line in the White Rose's letter to grandad: *The black mark on our sun is just the beginning of this thievery...*

"Yes," Yarrow confirmed, nodding. "The sun's energy is being stolen, at least that's what we think."

"And you said de energy disappeared in a specific spot..." Shelli furrowed her brow.

"Well yes, that's the other strange thing," Yarrow replied. "The temperature of one specific spot on the planet skyrocketed on both those occasions."

"Where?" Grian asked holding his breath.

"Quantum," Yarrow answered seriously.

Jeffrey gasped. "But Quantum is destroyed. There's nothing there!"

"Yes, that's what we've been told," Yarrow replied. "But we've been told a lot of things lately that have turned out not to be true."

CHAPTER 19

THE VISITOR

"But I don't understand... Are you...are you insinuating Quantum wasn't destroyed?" Jeffrey stuttered.

"I don't have a definitive answer," Yarrow said. "All I am saying for sure is we know that the vast amounts of solar radiation that disappeared on those two occasions seem to have done so over the city of Quantum. Beyond that, we don't know anything as fact. We do have people trying to investigate the city as we speak, but they are finding it impossible to gain access because of the exclusion zone."

"And do the Council believe that Howard Hansom is behind all this?" Jeffrey quizzed.

"We're not one hundred per cent sure," Yarrow replied, "but yes, many in the Council have surmised that it is Hansom – though of course again we have no definitive proof."

"Hansom said in the warehouse, when he was talking to Grandad, that he thought he was the saviour of humanity. He said something like...not everyone could get on the arch," Grian continued, a little uncertain of his memories.

"I imagine it's a Biblical reference. Perhaps he meant 'ark'?" Jeffrey suggested. "Wasn't there a religious story about a man named Noah, who built an ark and saved humanity and quite a lot of animals from a gigantic flood or some such?"

"So you think Hansom is building a boat to save de animals! He doesn't care about animals – look at his hForest—"

"No, Shelli, it's merely a metaphor for how Hansom might see himself. Perhaps he thinks he's like Noah!"

"So Hansom believes he's saving humanity..." Yarrow shook her head, confused. "That makes no sense. Surely Hansom knows you can't save anyone from a dying sun. Once the sun is gone, all nature – including us humans – will die with it."

"I think Hansom said nature was dying out for a long time before he'd started putting his plans in place." Grian shivered.

"Yeah, de Wilde say that too. Mother says nature was dying long before de black mark appeared on de sun. She says we'd lost so many species already."

"Well, Mother and Hansom are right," Yarrow said. "We humans have been destroying the planet for decades, and we were heading on a very bad trajectory if we didn't fix it. In fact, there was a lot of talk about how to fix what we were doing to the planet before the black mark appeared on the sun. But then the earthquake happened and the sun started disappearing and all that destruction accelerated drastically, until we got to where we find ourselves now – on the very brink."

"Did Hansom say who exactly he thinks he's saving or how he's saving them, Grian?" his dad asked. "If he really believes he's a saviour of humanity then we are clearly missing a much bigger part of this picture than we ever thought."

Grian shook his head as he tried desperately to remember Hansom's exact words the night he disappeared from the Tipping Point with Grandad.

"I mean could he think he's saving those volunteers? The people who signed up for the Tipping Point?" his dad continued.

"But why put them in cages and treat them the way he did then, Dad?" Grian asked, unable to forget how terrified his sister was when they found her. "They had no food or water. It didn't look like he was saving them."

"But ultimately he took them out of the cages and put them on the Hyperloop," Jeffrey replied, hopeful. "Is it possible he was bringing them somewhere nicer? Perhaps he's not all bad."

"You didn't hear him speak in the warehouse, Jeffrey. He *is* all bad." Grian sounded sharper than he'd meant.

A sudden knock on the main door interrupted their conversation. Everyone froze. Quickly, Yarrow ordered them all, except Vermilion, who'd just appeared in the kitchen, to hide.

Everyone scattered. Shelli raced for the fireplace in the sitting room area, while Jeffrey disappeared under the kitchen table.

The room was sparse and apart from those already used, there were very few places to hide. Grian panicked and jumped under a flower-printed blanket thrown on the couch, hoping whoever knocked on the door wouldn't come inside as he'd surely be seen.

Yarrow sat down on the couch beside him, pretending to read a book, as Grian held his breath and waited.

"Hello, officer," Vermilion said loudly.

Grian tensed even more.

"We're looking for a man and his three children. I've had a report that they might have passed this way. Have you seen them?" The policeman asked.

"No, I'm afraid not. It's just me and my partner," Yarrow replied cheerily, standing up.

"You're not locals. Are you staying here long?" the policeman probed further.

"Well spotted," Yarrow laughed. "We're actually touring around southern Babbage on holiday. We've only been in this quaint little town a few days. I'll be sure to give the station a call if I do see a man and his three children – did I get that bit right? I hope they're not dangerous!"

"Yes, that's right – a man, two boys and a girl. No, there's nothing to worry about. They're just people of interest. Everyone's on high alert these days. It's strange times, what with the sun and the accident in the Tipping Point..." The policeman sounded uncomfortable.

"Strange times indeed." Yarrow sighed. "Anyway, we promise to keep a lookout."

"Great," the policeman replied, "and enjoy your stay in Dunstan!"

The door closed and Grian waited a moment before jumping up.

"You've all got to go, now," Yarrow said quickly. "Go to the safe house in Hopper City. Zaffre is an old colleague of mine from the university. He will take you in. We'll follow on later tonight and should get there by the morning."

"But how will we get there?" Grian asked just as another knock rattled the door.

He ducked down on the couch and pulled the blanket roughly back in place. His heart thumped in his ears.

"It's me again," the policeman called, knocking once more.

"Just break the door down! I'm sure they're in there," a woman urged outside. She sounded like the librarian.

"Over here quick," Shelli whispered.

Grian pulled back the blanket. His friend had her rucksack in her hand and was standing by the whitewashed fireplace at the other side of the sitting room.

"We can climb up to the outside. It's easy," she said before ducking inside the chimney stack.

Grian raced over to the fireplace.

"Come on!" Shelli called, her voice muffled. "It's narrow and rough cut, so there's lots of foot holes. We'll be able to escape this way!"

"But Dad won't fit..." Grian panicked, looking around for his father.

"Just go, Grian. I'll be okay!" his dad pleaded, standing up from his hiding place behind the couch.

Jeffrey was next to disappear into the chimney after Shelli. Grian looked at his father, torn between staying and going.

"Go now! The safe house is at this location," Yarrow

163

urged, stuffing a note in Grian's hand.

"But, Dad, please?" Grian trembled, trying to hold himself together. "What if they—"

"There's no time! I promise I'll meet you in Hopper City. Now go," his father pleaded again, fear in his eyes.

A knock rattled the door once more.

"Just a minute!" Yarrow shouted, pushing Grian towards the fireplace.

He took one last look over his shoulder at his dad before climbing inside the chimney stack. He looked up and could see a circle of light blocked in part by the two dark outlines of his friends.

Another knock sounded on the door.

"Climb! Quick!" Shelli ordered from above.

CHAPTER 20

TRAPPED

Grian struggled up the chimney stack. His muscles ached and sweat raced down his forehead as he manoeuvred himself upwards in the tight space.

Shelli was already at the top and had just heaved Jeffrey out.

"Just a little more and I got ya, Grian," she encouraged, reaching down for him.

He strained for Shelli's outstretched hand. She grabbed his extended fingers then his wrist and pulled him upwards until he snaked out over the rim of the chimney.

He lay back breathless on a dusty clay hill, wheezing in the hot dry air. Dotted around him were the spaceship-like holes he'd seen yesterday. Now he was sure he knew what they were for. Some had to be the light wells for the cave-like homes below, while others were clearly chimney stacks.

Quickly he sat up, still breathless, and was about to speak when Shelli shook her head.

"Shush," she hushed, placing her ear to the ground. "There's something coming."

Across the clear desert plains, a large plume of sand appeared to be whirling towards them.

"I can pick up the vibrations. Something big is coming this way," she said. "I bet it's more police! We need to hide!"

The plumes of sand grew rapidly bigger, the cloud of dust almost blowing right into the edges of Dunstan now.

Grian spotted a small shack-like hut a short distance away. A large sign of a skull and crossbones hung on its battered wooden door, and a fence of barbed wire surrounded it.

"Over there," Grian said.

Thinking quickly, he slid down the hill and raced across to the hut.

"It looks quite uninviting," Jeffrey said, when he reached his friend.

"That makes it de best place to hide," Shelli replied, digging down in the loose sand with her hands to create a channel under the barbed wire fence. "Hurry. They're almost here."

Grian fell to his knees beside her and pulled out the last of the sand and stones before lifting up the bottom of the wire fence. Shelli was the first to scramble underneath, her T-shirt tearing on a barb. Grian followed behind, closing his eyes and mouth as the dust rose into his face before turning around to help Jeffrey through.

The clouds of moving dust had just engulfed the Dunstan sign and, emerging from the haze, floating along the half-hidden tarmac road into the town, was a fleet of large black jeeps and a black truck. All the vehicles had blacked-out windows.

"They're hHover vehicles – who would be driving those?" Jeffrey gasped, glancing back over his shoulder as Shelli yanked open the door of the hut and ushered them all inside.

The tight interior was stacked high with crates. Grian squeezed round them and snuck with Shelli across to a dirty plastic window. He was just in time to see people, shrouded in black cloaks, float out from the jeeps.

"Proctors!" he gasped, trembling. "They must be after us! Maybe one of the hSwarms saw us yesterday or..."

"Not possible," Jeffrey replied, pushing in for a look. "Why would Hansom deploy the Proctors in order to find us, when the police department and practically all of

Babbage are looking for us too – like he planned."

Just then, a man wearing the same dirty orange clothing Grian had seen on the miners yesterday moved in front of their line of vision. He began talking to one of the Proctors before pointing directly at the shed the kids were hiding in.

"We need to get out of here!" Grian panicked, feeling trapped. "They're coming this way. They must know we're here."

Shelli found a crack in one of the corrugated sheets at the back of the hut that was just big enough to crawl through. Quickly they scrambled outside before the door of the shed opened.

"It's getting harder to find this stuff, mate," a voice said. "I've the lads working night and day! With the amount you guys seem to be using, citrine's becoming as rare as gold!"

Grian looked at his friends, confused.

Through the crack he could see the miner switch on a naked bulb that hung from the low ceiling. The light fell on the dust that danced through the space, making it sparkle. Grian watched engrossed and afraid to even breathe. The miner reached into one of the crates and pulled out a yellow crystal just like the one Grian had seen in the shaft lift the day before.

Citrine. Yarrow had said that was what the White

Rose's crystal was made from. But Yarrow also said they didn't mine citrine in Dunstan, because it wasn't valuable. So why were there crate-loads of it in the hut? And why did the Proctors want it?

The Proctor flicked their wrist and the piece of citrine floated out of the miner's hand and began to spin slowly in the air in front of the pair, as if held by invisible string.

"It's...it's the genuine article," the miner stuttered, clearly nervous.

After a few taut seconds the Proctor flicked their wrist again and the rock zipped inside the arm of their oversized black cloak.

"Hey, you can't just take that!" The miner stepped forward, clearly annoyed. "We're still owed for the last batch. Times are tough, mate! The shop shelves are emptying and people here are worried. I need to pay my guys. Most of them have families. They've been working overtime for this lot!"

Without a word, the Proctor flicked their wrist again. This time the miner crashed up against the side of the shack and began to choke. The man squirmed and his face grew so red it looked like he might explode. Grian was rigid, petrified. He willed himself to look away but he couldn't. After what felt like ages, the miner spluttered and collapsed to the floor.

The Proctor swiped their hand again. This time some

of the crates hovered in the air. Then, with their gloved hand outstretched, the cloaked stranger manoeuvred the floating crates over the miner and out the door.

Grian looked round the side of the corrugated shack and watched the Proctor skilfully hover the stack of crates into the back of the waiting black truck.

"They're mining the same type of crystals as the one the White Rose sent to Grandad. They're obviously important!" Grian turned to his friends, his mind scrambling for answers while his heart raced. "We have to find out what Hansom needs the crystals for!"

Grian waited until all the Proctors were busy moving more crates from the hut. Then, impulsively, he slipped from hiding and raced for the truck, sneaking up into the cargo bed to hid behind the stacks of crates already moved inside.

"I really don't approve of this idea, Grian!" Jeffrey panted, swooping in beside him moments later.

"What are you two doing?" Grian gasped, as Shelli joined them too.

"Following you!" she spat. "We stick together. And poshy is right, this is not a good idea, Grian! What happened to having a plan!?"

The truck rocked and the three friends pulled further into hiding as another load of crates hovered up and were deposited onto the cargo bed.

"I just wanted to get one of these," Grian explained, grabbing a crystal from one of the crates. "To see why they're so special."

Quickly he closed his eyes and thought about Grandad. Nothing happened.

"They don't light up? Maybe they're not the same as the crystal the White Rose gave to Grandad," he whispered, opening his eyes again. "But Yarrow said the White Rose's crystal was citrine, and that miner said this one was citrine too. It can't be a coincidence!"

"Let me try," Shelli said grabbing one too and closing her eyes. Again, nothing happened.

"Well, they're clearly not the same composition," Jeffrey replied, a little pale and breathless. "These ones may be a variation of citrine. One that doesn't light—"

"Or maybe there's something else added to the White Rose's crystal and my Glimmer to make them glow. I can feel an energy off our two that I can't off these ones – but we can figure that out later," Shelli interrupted. "We need to get out of here, now!"

Suddenly the truck rocked again and a door slammed, as if someone had climbed into the front seat. Then daylight began to seep out of the cargo bed as the large rear door of the truck slid back into place.

"It appears it's too late to leave," Jeffrey whispered.

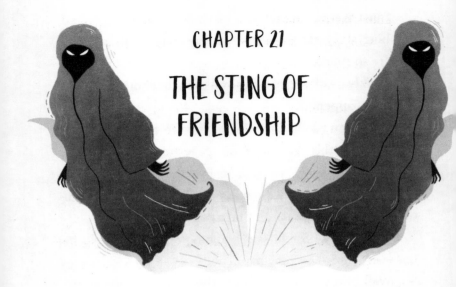

CHAPTER 21

THE STING OF FRIENDSHIP

The stacks of crates around them barely shifted as the truck lifted smoothly off the ground and began to move. Shelli lit up her Glimmer so they could see.

"Where do you think we're going?" Jeffrey whispered, the deep shadows on his face making him look a little scary.

"I don't know but it's my fault," Grian replied nervously. "I'm so sorry I got us all into this mess."

"Don't be silly, Grian," Jeffrey tutted, patting his friend's shoulder, "we've been in stickier situations together. I'm sure we'll figure something out."

"I bet we're going wherever it is these things are needed," Shelli said, picking up a crystal. "What do ya think they're using them for anyway?"

"Like Yarrow said, crystals are a pseudoscience," Jeffrey replied. "So I can't imagine what Howard Hansom would want with them. It's baffling!"

"A what science?" Grian asked.

"A pseudoscience – like homeopathy. It simply means not a *real* science."

"The Wilde always use homeopathy, and we're never sick!" Shelli sniped.

Now even Shelli was using words Grian didn't understand.

"Stop fighting, you two. Right at this minute it doesn't really matter what they're using the crystals for – we're stuck in the back of a Proctors' truck!"

"And who's fault is that?" Shelli glared.

Grian eyeballed her angrily, then looked away. The threesome slipped into an uncomfortable silence, the constant low hum of the engine the only background noise.

"I've been mulling over our predicament and come up with two options. Number one: we stay in the truck and find out why Hansom wants these crystals. It's risky though – I imagine wherever we're headed may be teeming with Proctors. Or number two: we find a way out of here, and get to that safe house Yarrow mentioned," Jeffrey eventually said, breaking the silence.

"I vote number two," Grian answered. "We can't get

173

distracted. Yarrow told us to go to the safe house. She'll meet us there in the morning with Dad and Vermilion. We need to help the Council solve the White Rose's puzzle and that starts with Dad's letter – otherwise we'll never save the world."

"How do hHovers work, Jeffrey?" Shelli asked out of the blue.

Jeffrey smiled, clearly keen to show his knowledge. "hHover vehicles can either be magnetic or glide on a cushion of air. The magnetic version needs specific magnet roads, such as in the Tipping Point. As these roads are not common in the rest of Babbage, I imagine these hHovers are air-cushion vehicles, or ACVs for short.

"Currents of slow-moving, low-pressure air are ejected downward, against the surface below the craft. Surrounding the base of the ACV is a flexible skirt, which traps the air currents, keeping them underneath the vehicle so it can move on any smooth surface, including land or water. Older ACVs were not energy efficient, they used substantial amounts of fuel and were slow, but Hansom redefined the vehicle with his new hPowerpacks."

"This skirt – what's it made of?" Shelli asked.

"Normally high-strength coated fabrics like neoprene or natural rubber," Jeffrey stated.

"Could it be pierced?" she continued.

"Theoretically yes, but ACVs can cope with small

piercings, they're designed for that."

"What about lots of small piercings?" Shelli raised her eyebrows this time.

Grian was about to say something when the truck swerved. He catapulted into the far corner of the cargo bed. Cowering, winded, he covered his head to avoid serious injury from the falling crates and crystals.

The truck swerved again, this time from side to side as if out of control.

"What's going on?" Grian cried.

Seconds later, he lurched forward, crashing painfully against a pile-up of crates as the vehicle stopped. Stunned, he was disentangling from the smash-up when a door slammed, and angry voices filled the air.

"What happened?" someone roared.

"I'm…I'm not too sure. I think the skirt blew out. It almost killed me!" a deep voice responded.

"Check on the cargo. The crystals can't be damaged or Hansom will have our lives."

Grian panicked, scrambling for a hiding place with Jeffrey as the back door slid open. Surely, they were going to be caught!

"Shelli!" he choked, spotting his friend in the middle of the truck facing the opening door. She looked fearless, her hands resting on her hips in superhero stance and muttering something over and over under her breath.

"What…who? What is going on?" one of Proctors stuttered when the door slid fully open.

Grian could clearly see his shocked expression, the hood of his cape resting over his shoulders.

Shelli didn't move.

"It's them – those kids Hansom told us to watch out for!" a caped woman cried, jumping out of a stopped jeep. She wasn't wearing her hood either.

Grian screamed at Shelli to move.

The woman pointed her arm, about to activate her hThoughtTech gloves, when she cried out and fell to the ground, clawing at her ankles.

For a moment everything stopped. Just like Grian, the other Proctors looked dumbfounded, staring at their fallen colleague who wriggled around in deep groans of pain.

"Run, now!" Shelli yelled, springing from the back of the truck onto the road.

She ducked under the arms of the first Proctor, who suddenly fell over screaming too.

Grian could see a tarmac road outside, its verge browned with sand. On one side of the road was an hForest. He jumped from the truck to follow Shelli.

All around him Proctors were falling like flies, gripping at their ankles or some other part of their body, screaming in agony.

One Proctor nearby tried desperately to wrench a large pin-like stick from his calf. Another Proctor, next to him, was on her knees, pulling at her face, which too was covered in the same large pins. Scurrying away from her at speed was a small furry animal. In fact, the same small furry animals were all over the road like a carpet of grey baubles.

Grian sprinted for the hForest which Shelli had disappeared into, jumping over a number of the small creatures on his way. He burst through the cover of the trees and kept running, only looking back when he heard a noise behind: Jeffrey was on his heels. The pair kept going until they saw Shelli ahead. Then Grian's concentration left him and he stumbled over a fallen branch in the middle of the undergrowth. As he lay on the ground, his lungs heaved, struggling for breath. His legs felt like jelly and he knew he couldn't run another step.

"What...what was...that? What happened...back... there?" he panted, looking around for Shelli.

His friend's eyes were closed and she stood, not even slightly panting, a little away from him, her back to a very large tree.

Something rustled out of the undergrowth and Grian startled. He sat quickly upright and shuffled backwards on his hands away from the small grey creature that stopped at Shelli's feet.

"She's one of my porcupine friends!" Shelli laughed,

bending down to carefully stroke the creature, whose back was full of the same large white and grey pins Grian had seen stuck in the Proctors. "Porcupines can throw their spikes a good distance, when asked nicely."

Grian lay back down on the ground and started to laugh too. Jeffrey joined in and by the time they'd finished, Grian's stomach ached from laughing so hard.

"What are we going to do now?" Jeffrey asked after they'd calmed down. "We haven't the slightest idea where we are. And the Proctors may well be on our tails..."

"We keep moving," Shelli said, standing up again. "The hForests are normally on de outskirts of towns or cities, so we must be near Hopper City."

Grian took the paper with the address Yarrow had given him from his pocket.

"Then let's find the safe house," he said.

CHAPTER 22
A WELCOME RETURN

Shelli looked up at the tops of the trees.

"Give me a second!" she said, before climbing the nearest trunk.

Grian watched in awe as she leaped from branch to branch along the treetops before finally disappearing into the foliage. Then just as quickly, she landed back down on the ground beside them.

"Hopper City appears to be that way." She pointed to her left. "De desert is behind us and de mountains just behind them. At least I think it's Hopper. There aren't any other cities out here far as I know?"

"Yes, Hopper is indeed the only city in this district," Jeffrey agreed. "The people of Hopper hold tightly to their city status, though many believe it's not big enough to be called a city at all."

"So, it's this way?" Grian said, pushing forward through the hum of digital trees.

He stopped as something rustled ahead. It was the afternoon and already growing dark in the hForest. Shelli lit up her Glimmer and kept walking. Grian stayed close behind her watching the shadows.

"Do you think the Proctors will follow us?" he asked, feeling a little jumpy.

"No," Shelli answered. "I think taking those crystals wherever they're meant to go is way more important to de Proctors than we are – especially when Hansom has de whole country looking for us anyway!"

"I wonder what he needs the crystals for..." Grian mused out loud, when more rustling ahead stopped him in his tracks.

He ducked down behind a tree, his heart pounding. Jeffrey quickly tucked in behind.

"Shelli, hide," Grian hissed, watching the hForest for the dark outline of a floating Proctor.

Shelli ignored him.

The rustling grew louder. Something was crashing through the undergrowth from the opposite direction towards them. Shelli started to run but she was running the wrong way.

"Shelli stop!" Grian called to warn her when she squealed and dropped her Glimmer.

The light went out.

"No!" Grian cried, stumbling forward out of hiding so fast he tripped over a tree stump.

He tumbled to the forest floor and lay winded, looking up at the canopy of trees, when Jeffrey appeared over him. His friend was in stitches.

"I am certain that fiasco would have gone viral if I had my Hansom to record it!" he laughed.

"But Shelli – where is she, what happened?" Grian asked confused.

"Panic averted. It was only Nach. The fox caught us."

Grian flipped over onto his stomach and sighed, relieved. Shelli was playing with her fox ahead. The Glimmer back in her hand highlighting Nach's deep red coat.

"But how did Nach find us?" Grian asked, standing up and dusting himself off.

"She's a tracker, like me!" Shelli answered, very pleased with herself as she walked back with Nach by her side.

"We're all together again – the Famous Four!" Jeffrey smiled. "A bit like those old children's adventure novels… though they were five."

"We're not famous," Grian grunted.

"Of course – you're right – the *infamous* four," Jeffrey said patting the fox's head.

"Right," Shelli said, the Glimmer illuminating the huge smile on her face. "Let's get going. Nach seems anxious, though, so we need to be careful."

They walked for a while, until Grian's stomach rumbled, shouting at him to eat.

"I'm starving," he complained after a bit.

Shelli reached into her rucksack for the bag Amergin had given them and handed them each an apple.

Grian didn't like apples, but right now it was the best thing he'd ever tasted. He limped forward, munching. His blistered feet were in pain – he winced as he walked around another tree stump and out onto a gravel path.

They appeared to be at the end of the hForest.

He stopped and looked up at the clear night sky. The stars shone bright from their deep navy canvas and Grian relaxed. The world seemed normal at night.

They were on a hill overlooking city lights, visible in the near distance.

"Hopper City," Jeffrey announced, his breath floating on the air. "A welcome sight."

"What's it like?" Grian asked.

"I have never been," Jeffrey replied, "but I have heard it's a step backwards in time. They still use old-fashioned trams. Apparently tourists love it for its antiquities."

"Right," Grian agreed absently. He'd gotten used to not understanding every word out of Jeffrey's mouth.

He walked forward and straight into Shelli's back. She had stopped dead on the track, Nach whimpering by her feet.

"What is it?" he asked, tensing up.

Shelli looked away and continued walking. Though she obviously didn't want him to, Grian had seen her tear-filled eyes.

"I imagine she's upset about those," Jeffrey whispered, pointing across to a collection of felled trees at the side of the road. "They must be expanding the hForest."

Grian caught up to his friend. Unsure what to say to make it any better, he stayed in silence beside her.

"Sometimes I think if we tried to destroy all of nature," Shelli spoke, a little later, "nature would still survive. It's just probably us humans that wouldn't."

"I don't like it when you say things like that!" Grian sighed. "I want to survive, and I want my family to survive too. Unlike you, I actually like humans!"

"So do I, Grian!" Shelli barked, her pain replaced by anger. "Mother says we are nature and if we work with nature to protect it, we protect ourselves. Trees, animals, plants, insects, humans – we are all de same thing. Yous'll see. As de sun dies everything will die with it, including us, because everything is connected."

"I imagine it can be done... Working with nature, that is," Jeffrey piped up from behind them. "Though I'm not sure where the profit would be in it. Business makes the world go round, and a successful business needs profit."

"Maybe being alive might be de profit, poshy!" Shelli snapped furiously, before storming ahead down the gravel track.

All three descended into a prickly silence as they wound their way towards the city. Grian really liked his friends, but sometimes he needed a break from talking, and from all the other worries of the world. He took out Yarrow's note and looked at the address again.

First, they had to find the safe house, so they could help the Council work towards solving the White Rose's puzzle. Because if they didn't save the sun, nothing else really mattered.

CHAPTER 23

THE SAFE HOUSE

Grian watched Nach trot ahead of him, her brush-like tail swishing gently behind her. After a while, the gravel path wound down onto a quiet, narrow road lined on both sides with tall lamp posts that cast pools of bright white light on the tarmac. As the sky was pitch dark, Grian imagined it must have been around eight or nine at night, but with the sun dying and without his Hansom, it was hard to tell what time of the day or night it was any more.

Grian pulled his *Dunstan Dinos* baseball cap down further on his head as they got closer to the city, hyper-aware that most of Babbage was on the lookout for them now.

Soon housing estates began to appear off either side of the road. Grian took out the piece of paper Yarrow had given him again. He'd never been to Hopper City, so the address meant nothing. He really wasn't sure how they were going to find the safe house.

"I propose we knock on doors," Jeffrey said, echoing Grian's tentative thoughts. "It's an old-fashioned approach to wayfinding, but I imagine it's effective."

"But what if someone recognizes us?" Grian shuddered.

"Look." Shelli pointed to a rectangular beacon of light in the distance. "Isn't that one of those interactive map things?"

"Brilliant," Jeffrey announced, already racing ahead.

"We're looking for Hopper Heights, number thirty-three," Grian panted, stopping in front of the large, illuminated map.

"Hopper Heights is two point one kilometres from here," the map announced, then a bright-blue line lit up on screen, highlighting the way. "It's approximately a twenty-three-minute walk at medium pace."

"I won't remember these directions," Grian whispered, trying to memorize the unfamiliar street names.

"Fortunately for you both," Jeffrey smiled, tapping a finger on the side of his head, "I have a photographic memory!"

"You have told us that before," Grian teased, "so

maybe your memory isn't as good as you think it is!"

Then Grian choked. An advert caught his eye in the stream of advertisements displayed along the side of the interactive map.

The double H logo of the Hansom brand sat at the top of the ad above the word *WANTED* in bright-red letters. Below the red letters were cut-outs of Grian, Shelli and Jeffrey from the shoulders up like they were movie stars. A moment later their heads dissolved into the background before the sentence: *ONE MILLION BABCOIN REWARD* popped out.

"A million babcoins… Oh my, I'd nearly give myself up for that amount!" Jeffrey stated.

Grian laughed out loud, the seriousness of the situation washed away on his friend's remark. Shelli joined in and eventually Jeffrey until the threesome were in hysterics. They only managed to stop when Shelli spotted an elderly couple staring at them from across the street.

"I think we better go before we draw too much attention." She nudged Grian in the ribs.

Jeffrey led them off in silence, turning down roads with confidence until they came to large pillars marking the entrance to an estate. The words *Hopper Heights* were engraved onto a plaque by one of the pillars.

Every house in Hopper Heights looked exactly the same; each one had the same red-brick facade and white-framed windows. And there were a lot of houses, packed tightly around small green areas down every road they walked. Grian wondered how anyone would ever find their way home without a Hansom.

"There – number thirty." Shelli pointed across yet another green. "Thirty-three must be near."

They raced over the neatly mowed grassy centre and searched the other side of the street until they came to a rich-blue door, 33 glistening in raised gold numbers under a bright porch light.

They looked at each other, but no one knocked.

"Can we trust Yarrow?" Shelli whispered, voicing Grian's concern.

Before either could answer, the front door opened inward a little. A man with a long, thin face and large protruding ears, like butterfly's wings, poked his head out through the narrow opening. He looked suspiciously around before opening the door fully and ushering them quickly inside. He didn't even flinch when Nach followed after them.

"I've a camera, you see. It's on my doorbell and it has saved me many times from unwanted guests. You, of course, are welcomed – by me at least, if not by the rest of Babbage. I've seen your faces on the news. You're Adler's grandson, if I'm not mistaken?!" The man spoke quickly, looking curiously at Grian.

"Yes," Grian replied, nodding. "Yarrow sent us."

"Oh my – Yarrow… Well, in that case you better come into the drawing room. I gather we have much to discuss."

The man walked down an ornate hall to a gold-painted door. The hall was wallpapered in colourful exotic birds peeping out behind large golden leaves. Hanging from the ceiling of the hall was a crystal chandelier, dripping in coloured glass fruit, and along the walls hung gold-framed illustrations of butterflies.

He pushed open the door of the drawing room and lead them inside.

This room was painted black and dominated by a huge black marble fireplace. Gold-framed glass boxes filled every centimetre of hanging space.

Each glass box held a different type of butterfly, its delicate wings pinned open. A small card sat bottom centre of every glass box with the word *Species* typed above long names Grian couldn't pronounce and that he wasn't even sure were in English.

He stared in amazement at a green butterfly with a small red dot on each of its wings, trying to work out how the word *Gonepteryx rhamni* sounded, when their host spoke.

"Latin can be a tongue-twister. At least, it was for me when I first began my studies."

Grian turned around. The man was tall and thin, just

like his face and wore a suit of deep purple velvet.

"Take a seat." He pointed a long, elegant finger at a yellow couch beside the fireplace.

Grian popped down between his friends, who were already seated on the couch. Shelli was rigid, and looked furious as she eyed the glass boxes that hung from the walls all around the room.

"I see you've spotted my butterfly friends," the man commented to her, smiling.

"How can these be your friends! They're all dead," she growled, as Nach, who'd been lying at her feet, lifted her head from her black paws and pricked her ears, sensing her friend's unease.

"Well, I assure you, young lady, I source all my beautiful friends ethically. They were dead when I purchased them. All died of natural causes – reached the end of their life cycle, so to speak. We will all reach the end of our glorious life cycle and find ourselves on another adventure someday of course. I hope to come back as a bird. Imagine soaring on the winds, high above this wondrous planet! And if someone finds my mortal body beautiful enough to put in a glass box and hang on their wall, I know my soul would sing in celebration."

"Well my soul wouldn't," Shelli sniped.

"So you're on the Council of—" Grian interjected, just before Shelli elbowed him in the ribs and shook her head.

He stopped speaking abruptly, a little red-faced and sore.

"Ah, I see! Of course, you do need to be cautious when all of Babbage is vying for your blood," the man noted, before pulling out a small pin from inside the breast pocket of his suit.

The pin was of a colour wheel. The same as the one Yarrow wore.

"So you are a Council member? This is the safe house?" Grian questioned.

"Yes, my name is Zaffre! Now you haven't yet told me why Yarrow sent you. She is my dearest of friends. How she is?"

"We met her in Dunstan," Grian answered. "We were hiding out with her and Vermilion and my dad, but the librarian spotted us and we had to get away. Yarrow gave us your address. She said she'll be here in the morning with the others."

"How did you get into de Council?" Shelli raised her eyebrows. "I didn't think they'd let someone in who pinned dead butterflies inside glass cages."

"Oh my dear, you are a prickly one, but I like your spunk. I'm an entomologist – quite renowned I'll have you know – I study insects. And, as I said, these butterflies are all my friends..."

Grian's stomach grumbled loudly. It sounded a lot like

a washing machine, and suddenly all he could think about was food.

"I hear you're hungry... I'm sure being on the run must do that!" Zaffre stood up. "I have been known to host the odd tea party. I'll just whip something up and be right back."

As Zaffre left, Grian got up and explored the room to distract himself from the rumblings in his belly.

A recessed glass cabinet in the far corner was filled with books. All the books looked old and worn, with delicate gold lettering on faded fragile spines.

As he scanned the shelves, one of the titles drew him in.

Aztecs: The Five Suns.

A shiver raced across his shoulders. Yarrow said she'd thought the jaguar sun in the White Rose's riddle had something to do with an ancient tribe called the Aztecs!

He opened the cabinet door and pulled out the book, which was wedged tightly between its neighbours.

On the cover was a picture of a strange circular stone-carved face with a protruding tongue.

Grian opened the contents page and skimmed down before almost dropping the book in shock.

Chapter three was titled *The First Sun – Jaguar*.

CHAPTER 24

THE FIRST SUN

"What is it, Grian?" Jeffrey asked, concerned.

"You have to see this... You really have to see this," Grian stuttered excitedly.

He raced over and sat on the couch beside his friends. Jeffrey grabbed the book from his hands and was studying the cover when Grian forced open the contents page and stabbed at chapter three with his finger.

"Look! The jaguar sun! Yarrow was right, it does have something to do with the Aztecs."

"Umm," Jeffrey said, looking back up at his friend. "I'm afraid, Grian, it doesn't say 'jaguar sun'. It in fact says 'The First Sun – Jaguar'. It's an entirely different thing."

"Let me see." Shelli snatched the book from Jeffrey and flicked through the pages until she reached chapter three.

"According to Aztec mythology," she read from the book, "de creator couple gave birth to four sons, and these gods began to create de universe, including de creation of cosmic time called 'suns'. After de world was created, de gods gave life to humans but in order to do this they had to sacrifice themselves. De first god to sacrifice himself was called Tezcat…Tezcatl…Tezcat… I don't know what any of this means!"

"Tezcatlipoca," Jeffrey corrected, looking at the text over her shoulder. "And it's Aztec mythology, it's not necessary that we know what it means, only how it relates to solving the White Rose's puzzle…"

"Oh, hold on, look at this bit," Shelli said urgently. "'Tezcatlipoca leaped into de fire and started de first sun, called de jaguar sun.'"

"See – the jaguar sun!" Grian jumped up in excitement just as Zaffre returned to the room, his arms laden with a packed tray of sandwiches and tea.

"What's going on here?" he asked, raising a pointed eyebrow as he set the tray down on a low coffee table.

Grian turned around quickly to face the man. "It's, ahem…it's just…" He hesitated, looking at his friends for guidance.

"I appreciate that you don't want to share information with me. And you are of course right to be cautious. These are indeed strange times. All I can do is promise on the graves of my departed loved ones, of which I have many, that I am a friend."

"We think Grian may have found a clue to a puzzle we're trying to solve," Jeffrey mumbled, having already stuffed a sandwich into his mouth.

"And what is this puzzle?" Zaffre asked tentatively.

"It was written in a letter from the White Rose," Grian replied.

"Oh my," Zaffre gasped, his hand flying straight to his mouth. "So it's true, those letters are not just a cruel rumour set to break all our hearts?"

"No," Grian shook his head, "the letters are real. The Postal Network found one and Dad took it to Yarrow."

Grian and the others filled Zaffre in on all that had happened in the Tipping Point, and everything that had taken place since. The only piece they left out was any mention of Grandad's letter or the crystal.

"Well, after that I really could do with a stiff drink," Zaffre admitted. He shook his head and took the book on the Aztecs from Grian's hand to thumb through it.

Grian reached for another sandwich.

"Yes, I remember reading about this years ago. I love the Aztecs, you see, because they loved butterflies almost as much as I do. They believed butterflies were reservoirs for the souls of soldiers killed on the battlefield. It's both sad and heroic all at once, don't you think? The Aztecs, I'm sure you know, are an ancient civilization of sun worshippers, so it would seem fitting that the White Rose mentioned them in this puzzle."

"They're not exactly mentioned. I wish I could remember how the puzzle goes exactly..." Grian shook his head, frustrated.

"It's okay, Grian," Jeffrey mumbled, his mouth once again full of bread. "I believe I can recite it in full."

Jeffrey swallowed his sandwich before clearing his throat, and launching into the poem.

"Dear Postman,
Only the Poet can see,
What's truly reflected in me,
I'm precious to the night sky,
Of my majesty I am not shy.
For I'm as black as the jaguar sun,
And in my heart the battle is won.
The White Rose."

"Oh wow. Now that was written by a master," Zaffre said, rubbing his forehead. "There is definitely a link to the Aztecs in that riddle, not only in the jaguar sun but also in the mention of the night sky. If my memory serves me correctly, the night sky is somehow related to the jaguar sun…"

Without another word, Zaffre rose from his seat and stepped out of the sitting room. The stairs in the hallway creaked, then there were footsteps in a room above their heads. A few minutes later, he returned, hidden behind a stack of books.

He doled out a few books each to Shelli, Grian and Jeffrey.

"Can everyone read?" Zaffre asked.

They all nodded.

"Well, you can't presume anything these days. All these smart devices have made a generation helpless. But then again, some of the smartest people I know can't decipher the written word. And what is language? Only something we made up to communicate with one another when, honestly, we'd probably be far better off if we'd never invented a word!"

Then the man sat down in his seat and picked a book from the remaining pile.

"We're looking for any reference to 'night sky', especially in relation to the jaguar sun," he told them. "I know it's in one of these books. I just can't recall which one."

Grian was daunted by the five thick books on the floor

beside him. He never read books in school; Bob always did it for him while Grian usually nodded off.

The first book he picked up was called *A History of Aztec Mythology* and the words were so small on the page his eyes glazed over.

He flicked to the page of contents, hoping something would jump out but nothing did. He glanced at Shelli. She was concentrating so hard, her nose almost touched the page she studied. Jeffrey was halfway through his first book already, and Zaffre was busy speed-reading the page in front of him.

"Don't you have a hTablet or something I could use? It'd be much quicker," Grian asked.

"Oh no, I have nothing that's connected to the hNet." Zaffre's eyebrows furrowed above the bright-yellow glasses he'd just popped on. "Everything digital is trackable, you know. All the Council have gotten rid of their devices. If I need the hNet, I have a place I can go. Books are much safer and I, fortunately, have lots of them."

"I think I have something," Shelli suddenly piped up. "This paragraph says Tez...cat...lipoca – that's de God in your book, Grian! – ruled over de jaguar sun, de Great Bear constellation and de night sky..."

"That is amazing work, Shelli!" Zaffre applauded, beaming. "So that connects the night sky and the jaguar sun both mentioned in the riddle. Clearly the White Rose is pointing us in the direction of the Aztecs."

"What's truly reflected in me..." Grian said, repeating aloud a line from the riddle. "The 'me' in that line has to be what the White Rose wants us to find, don't you think? The word 'reflected' makes me think of a river or a mirror or something like that."

"Well, now that you mention mirrors, Grian, perhaps I have found a third connection between the riddle and the Aztecs." Jeffrey smiled, looking up from his book. "This book says the name Tezcatlipoca is often translated in Nahuatl, the Aztec language, as 'smoking mirror' and alludes to the god's connection to obsidian. Obsidian is the material from which mirrors were made in Aztec times—"

"Oh my," Zaffre interrupted. Suddenly pale, he repeated another line from the riddle. *"I'm precious to the night sky!* So we're looking for a mirror that is precious to the Aztecs...and I think I know exactly where it is!"

CHAPTER 25
THE BLACK MIRROR

"What? Where?" Grian asked excitedly.

Zaffre suddenly moved to his knees and began rifling quickly through papers that were piled up on a shelf underneath the coffee table beside him.

"It's here somewhere – not the mirror, of course, I don't have that here. I'm sure I read it only recently. I wouldn't have thrown it out. I'm a member of the royal museum, you see. In fact, I'm a patron. I even sat on their board for a stint," he rambled.

"What is he talking about?" Shelli asked, confused.

"He's acting rather odd – do you think he's okay?" Jeffrey whispered, looking a little concerned.

Grian couldn't help but smile at Jeffrey's concern.

Zaffre seemed to him like an adult version of his friend.

"Ah! Here we go." The man looked relieved as he pulled out a thin glossy booklet.

On the cover of the booklet the letters *RSM* were superimposed over a picture of a happy family staring in amazement at a virtual giant dinosaur skeleton.

"I always wanted to visit the RSM, but I haven't been so keen since the museum relocated to Hopper City. The original one in Quantum appeared to be much more impressive," Jeffrey stated.

"What are you talking about? What is the RSM?" Grian asked, feeling a little frustrated.

"It's the Royal Science Museum," Zaffre answered, waving the booklet around. "And this is the new schedule advertising what's on at the museum. I distinctly remember reading something about an old Aztec mirror that fascinated me…"

He fell quiet studying the booklet.

"Here we go." He looked up in delight moments later. "There is a visiting John Dee exhibition—"

"Who's John Dee?" Shelli interrupted.

Zaffre held up a hand and began to read from the page.

"The mathematician John Dee had a reputation as a scholar… Blah blah…" the man said, skimming the article. "But he was notoriously known for his conversations with angels. These conversations, for him, were as viable a method as maths for understanding the natural world, and he carried out these conversations using his scrying object…"

"What's a scrying object?" Grian asked, trying to understand what was being read.

"Scrying is the ability to tell the future by talking to spirits. A scrying object is what one might use to scry, such as a crystal ball or mirror," Zaffre replied. "Now hold on… Yes, here it is… Dee used a black obsidian Aztec mirror for scrying. Many at the time thought Dee mad, of course, but he was such a good mathematician they ignored his eccentricities."

"He was certainly eccentric," Jeffrey commented. "There is no scientific proof for spirits or angels!"

Zaffre tutted. "A true scientist must indeed have the most open of minds, Jeffrey – especially in a field we know nothing about."

"Do you think this mirror might be what the White Rose wants us to find? You said you know where it is?" Shelli encouraged.

"Yes, yes, yes…" Zaffre was now overly excited, his voice elevated up a pitch. "Here it is – the best bit. An anonymous donor has recently donated John Dee's black Aztec scrying spirit mirror to the museum!"

"Yes!" Grian whooped excitedly, before reciting another line from the riddle, "*Of my* majesty *I am not shy.*

You said that museum is called the Royal Science Museum. Majesty, royal...it fits!"

"And de mirror was donated recently by an anonymous donor... Maybe de donor was de White Rose!" Shelli jumped from her seat. "It has to be what we're looking for..."

"Certainly it all fits," Zaffre said, raising an eyebrow. "But I have just one question. How do you know the White Rose wants us to find anything?"

Grian turned, a little red-faced. He'd handed the first letter, the one Grandad had given him, to Yarrow. In it, the White Rose said that each of the four letters leads to a piece of a bigger puzzle and that the crystal that came with Grandad's letter was the first piece. So this black mirror was possibly the second piece. But Grian couldn't tell Zaffre that – Grandad's letter was a secret; he could only share it with Yarrow. It was up to Yarrow to decide who else she wanted to know about it.

"I'm beginning to think there may be some things you three know that I'm not privy to. I don't mind. I would prefer not to be privy to a lot of things, if I'm honest. Especially what is happening in our world right now. In fact, if I could, I would climb into a chrysalis and come out a beautiful butterfly, when the world has been healed. But alas, we must endure..."

Zaffre sighed, glancing out the window at the night.

"In saying that, I will make myself available to help in whatever way necessary, if you really believe we must get this mirror. Though I have to admit I have never committed robbery in my life and I haven't a notion how one might go about it."

"There's someone I'm acquainted with who may be able to help us in that regard, and I'm almost certain they live in Hopper City," Jeffrey said, smiling. "But there is a slight problem. To contact them I really need to access the hNet, to go through my IRC channel…"

"What's an IRC channel?" Shelli asked.

"Internet Relay Chat," Jeffrey answered. "It's a tech thing."

"Are you sure you really need the hNet?" Zaffre sounded hesitant.

Jeffrey nodded, definite. "Yes, it's imperative."

"Okay." Zaffre stood up. "Let me grab my coat. It's late so there shouldn't be anyone about the streets. I'll take you to Giga Bite."

CHAPTER 26
GIGA BITE

"What is Giga Bite?" Shelli whispered, walking behind Zaffre out of the estate and down a small hill, passing shops and restaurants that were long closed up for the night.

"I don't know," Grian replied, watching Zaffre approach one of the only places on the quiet street that appeared to be open.

Over the door of the premises hung a sign that read *GIGA BITE CAFE* in large neon-green letters. The place looked dark inside except for odd flashes of blue light.

Zaffre opened the door and an electronic bell sounded as they stepped inside the café onto a central aisle that ran up to a reception desk. Both sides of the aisle were lined with narrow booths. Each booth contained a large gaming chair, facing a widescreen hTV mounted to the wall.

"Oh my, a gaming café! This is rather old-school," Jeffrey whispered, excited.

Most of the booths were full, with people wearing hEarPods and intensely playing computer games as if nothing else existed. No one noticed the small group walking the aisle to the graffiti-covered reception desk at the back.

A large man in an oversized black T-shirt looked up briefly from his screen behind the desk to nod at Zaffre. Then Zaffre pulled a neon green loyalty card from his suit pocket and swiped it against a small payment unit before moving to the nearest empty booth.

"Can you access what you need from here?" he whispered to Jeffrey.

Jeffrey pulled out the chair and quickly sat down.

"I'll open a game first so it doesn't look suspicious," he muttered, more to himself than the others.

Jeffrey launched "Beat the Barber", one of Grian's favourite computer games, before opening a smaller hNet window in the bottom corner of the monitor. He typed in something on the keypad and a black screen with a list of different coloured text appeared.

[23:43]   *boygirl2 has quit

[23:43]   *beanbagbunny75 has joined.

[23:43]   *jolyjef5 has joined.

[23:44]   jolyjef5
Mushka need to speak to u.
Private channel.

Then a second window opened, which looked the same as the first only this one was empty.

[23:44]   mushka
what's up J - bzy here.

[23:44]   jolyjef5
need ure help. In hopper. Police on my tail.

[23:45]   mushka
ha ha - ya right. later

[23:45.18]   jolyjef5
serious. watch news. J slight. mayb u were rite
about tipping point

[23:45]   mushka

news? Serious? J slight u? Nevr...

[23:45]   jolyjef5

yes. do bkground check. Its me. Need help. Urgent.

[23:45]   mushka

where u now?

[23:46]   jolyjef5

in a cafe - giga bite.

"No, Jeffrey!" Zaffre hissed, gripping the back of the gaming chair. "It's a rule of the Council's, you never give out that kind of information. What were you thinking!?"

"It's fine, I assure you," Jeffrey dismissed him. "Mushka can be trusted."

Grian didn't feel as confident as his friend. A bang shook the floor in the room above their heads. It sounded as if something had fallen over. He stiffened and looked around nervously. No one else seemed to have noticed, all too engrossed in whatever game it was they were playing.

[23:48]   jolyjef5

mushka - are u still there?

Grian gulped. His heart pounded, watching the screen waiting for a reply. Jeffrey began to tap his fingers on the desk in front of him. Was he nervous now too?

[23:51]   jolyjef5
hello? Mushka I need ur help. U owe me.

Grian's skin grew itchy – they needed to leave. One of the gamers across the aisle shifted uncomfortably in his seat and whispered something into his Hansom.

"We have to go – Mushka could have called the police by now. We'll be trapped in here," he whispered, pulling on his friend's arm.

Jeffrey kept staring at the screen as if waiting for something to happen. He typed one last message to Mushka, when a reply spontaneously appeared.

There was a slight ripple of unease as they all four leaned forward to read it.

[23:55]   *mushka has quit

Jeffrey looked shocked. He sat unmoving, staring at the screen while Shelli almost lifted him from his chair. Zaffre was already at the door and had slipped outside under the sound of the bell.

"I...I don't understand," Jeffrey stuttered. "Mushka

wouldn't tell the police. I've helped him out on numerous occasions in the past when he was in trouble with the law, and I have incriminating evidence on him. It's how hackers keep loyalty. He was the most-wanted boy in Babbage – before you, Grian, or me, that is – and unlike you and me, he was wanted for quite legitimate reasons, some might say—"

"It doesn't matter. We just need to leave now," Grian hissed, trying not to make a scene pushing his friend towards the café door.

They rushed out into the chilly night air. Grian shivered, though he was sure it wasn't from the cold.

Zaffre stood under a street light, his shadow stretching like a thin pencil across the path. "That was reckless. We'll take a different route home," he said, glaring at Jeffrey, who still looked shocked.

They set off quickly, no one speaking and were a little up the road when an electronic beep sounded in the silent street behind them. Grian looked round, the hairs on the back of his neck now upright. The street was deserted, but a robotic voice filled the air.

"*Read the bus sign*," the voice said. It sounded like it was coming from a tiny speaker high in a lamp post nearby.

"I knew it – Mushka would not abandon me!" Jeffrey clapped, racing over to a bright bus stop on the other side of the quiet road.

Grian followed and watched in amazement when the large screen of the bus stop, which normally showed adverts and bus times, went blank. Then all of a sudden across its black face the sentences *Go round to the back of Giga Bite café. Knock on the blue door four times. And wait.* were displayed. Then abruptly the screen went blank again.

Grian shivered and crossed back across the road after Jeffrey, who was heading straight for the café.

"What did it say?" Shelli asked, grabbing Jeffrey's arm.

"To go round the back of the café," Grian replied, uneasy.

"Shouldn't we think about this? How do you know it's Mushka? And even if it is, how do you know we can trust them? They're a wanted hacker. It might be best we go," Zaffre insisted.

"I think we should follow him," Shelli replied. "Jeffrey hasn't let us down before."

Zaffre nodded and followed the others. They slipped quickly along a short alleyway and round to a green paint-chipped door at the back of Giga Bite.

"Step forward to the doorbell and place your left eye in front of the peephole," the robotic voice spoke again – this time it appeared to come from a little black speaker stuck to the door.

In the middle of the door was what looked like a

doorbell with a spyhole on the top. Jeffrey stepped forward first, and a small blue laser light darted across his eyeball.

"A retina scanner," the boy gushed in awe.

"What's that?" Shelli asked.

"It's for biometric verification."

Grian was about to ask a question when all of a sudden there was a faint click and the green door opened inwards.

"*Step in, Jeffrey,*" the robotic voice ordered.

Jeffrey stepped inside and was just looking back at the others, a large smile on his face, when the door banged closed.

"What? No!" Grian panicked.

"*Next,*" the robotic voice said.

"I'm the adult here, let me go," Zaffre said to Grian and Shelli. "I'll sort this out."

The tall man walked forward and stooped a little to reach the peephole. His eye was scanned, and it was watering when he stepped away. Then the door opened and Zaffre went inside. Again, it banged closed behind him.

Grian and Shelli were alone in the street.

"*Next,*" the voice ordered once more.

"What do you think?" Grian asked.

"I don't know – Jeffrey seems to trust this Mushka person," Shelli reasoned, Nach growling slowly at her feet.

"But Jeffrey trusts everyone!" Grian argued.

"Maybe we should trust him though," Shelli replied.

"*Next,*" the robotic voice said once more.

"Argh, okay – I'm coming!" Shelli snapped, approaching the scanner.

The blue laser light flashed across her eye and the door opened. Shelli gulped, looking back at Grian one more time before stepping slowly inside. Nach had just managed to snake in through her legs when the door closed again.

Grian was left in the dark alleyway alone. Something scuttled past in the shadows and he jumped. It was probably a cat, he persuaded himself, though goosebumps still rose up on his arms.

"*Next,*" the voice said again.

He took a deep breath and walked forward, blinking uncomfortably when the blue ray scanned past his eye. He rubbed it, stepping back.

His heart thumped and it felt like ages before there was a click. The door opened inwards.

Grian stepped inside the entrance hall. Straight in front of him was a staircase, the steps highlighted in green neon strips. The rest of the entrance hall was painted black and appeared to be empty of any furniture or decoration.

His friends were waiting halfway up the staircase in

the semi-dark. Their faces were cast in a green hue so they looked a little like zombies from "The Living Zead", another computer game Grian used to play.

"What's going on?" he whispered, looking up at them.

"We were told to wait here," Jeffrey whispered back.

Suddenly a dark figure appeared at the top of the stairwell.

"Welcome to my lair," the person said.

CHAPTER 27

MUSHKA

"We're here to see Mushka," Jeffrey spoke with confidence. "Can you please take us to him? It's urgent!"

Their host stepped forward into the green light, revealing themselves.

The girl was small. Her face hidden behind a curtain of ear-length hair that was purple-tipped, though it was hard to tell under the green light. She wore a black beanie, a black T-shirt of a wolf baring its teeth, and a pair of torn black jeans.

She squinted at Jeffrey for a few seconds before speaking again.

"He is not here!"

"We need his help," Jeffrey insisted, as the girl

narrowed her eyes. "I made contact. I presumed you were bringing us to him. Howard Hansom set us up, the sun is dying and we need Mushka's help to rectify the situation. I must insist you get him!"

"Ha! I knew Hansom was up to something. So it is dying... Wow, like, that's pretty major! How do you know that, though?"

"I don't mean to be rude," Jeffrey said, "but this information is strictly confidential. We can only impart it to Mushka."

"You don't mean to be rude, but you're being pretty rude Jef! Just go. I'll tell Mushka to find you – he's good at that," the girl huffed, before turning away to push open a door off the landing.

"No, stop..." Shelli stumbled up the stairs to the top. "Please ignore Jeffrey – sometimes he is clueless. We really need your help!"

Jeffrey looked from Shelli back to the girl, totally confused.

"I'm pretty sure *she's* Mushka!" Shelli hissed at him under her breath.

Grian tried not to laugh when Jeffrey's mouth dropped open. The girl stopped and held open the door she had just been about to walk through.

"Fine... Follow me," she said, disappearing inside.

The room they walked into was also dark and painted

black, just like the hallway. All three walls in front of them were covered in screens of various sizes. Some of the screens were mounted to the walls while others rested on a variety of different desks, creating a wide U-shaped workspace. A chair on wheels sat in the middle of the U. It had large armrests, each with a panel that looked like a mouse pad. Over the back of the chair, hanging from the headrest, was a work ID card on a lanyard for *Giga Bite Café*. It had a picture of Mushka over the name *Ava Thompson*.

Mushka growled and swiped the card away when she saw Grian looking at it. He smiled to himself – her real name was a total contrast to her character.

Then she sat on the four-wheeled chair and pushed herself across the room to a set of screens on the left wall. She clicked the mouse panel. Grian startled when pictures of him, Shelli, Jeffrey and Zaffre appeared on the screens beside what looked like enlarged images of their eyes.

"You're looking at my security check. I scanned your retinas on these images I found and compared them to the door scans. I mean, a girl's got to know if you are who you say you are. And you are, you all check out," she said over her shoulder.

"So, ahem, you're actually Mushka. It's…it's nice to finally catch up," Jeffrey stuttered, looking properly rattled for the first time since Grian met him. "I'm sorry I failed to recognize you. I met you – well, I mean, I thought I met you at Comic Con – but—"

"They let you into Comic Con!?" the girl sneered, without cracking a smile.

Jeffrey blushed. Grian could almost feel the heat off him.

"Please. We need your help," Shelli cut in.

"You know you guys are all over the media." Mushka pressed a button and every screen in the room filled with a different hNews channel.

Every channel appeared to be airing a version of the same story, about how they'd destroyed the Tipping Point.

"It's not safe that you're here. There's a reward, one million babcoin. Not to be sniffed at!"

"We heard," Shelli replied steadily. "But if ya are what Jeffrey says ya are, then ya know it's all lies. We're trying to save de sun and we need your help."

Mushka didn't miss a beat. "Is this something to do with the White Rose?"

"What do you know about that?" Grian asked, sounding harsher than he'd meant.

"Nothing, except that Howard Hansom's desperate for information on them. I was monitoring the Tipping Point and Hansom for a while before the explosion in the TP.

Something wasn't right about that whole setup. A friend of mine moved there with her family. She was always on social but her posts stopped and I couldn't get in contact with her. Others said the same things about their family members, so let's say I started to investigate.

"A while before the explosion you guys are meant to have set, Hansom let his guard down a little. He was panicked about some White Rose and letters – worried whoever they were would stop his plans."

"What exactly are his plans?" Grian's heart pounded.

"Were – he's presumed dead, remember." She winked.

"He's not dead," Grian continued. "He faked it all, just like he faked the Tipping Point. He's still alive, I'm sure of it!"

"Huh. Well, I thought as much. He's giving off serious BBEG vibes!" Mushka said, not at all surprised.

"What is BBEG?" Grian whispered to Jeffrey.

"Big Bad Evil Guy," Mushka replied loudly. "Haven't you ever played 'Dungeons and Dragons'? It's my life! So yeah, I don't know Hansom's plans. He never talked specifics – he was careful online and with hMail. But his plans did have something to do with the sun. Jef said it's dying…?"

"Yes, we think so," Zaffre replied. "That's the conclusion the Council have come to."

"You're the Council of Colour! I've seen some of the

Council's published papers." Mushka nodded at Zaffre. "They are, like, mind blowing. I've tried to track your members, just to see if you guys are legit. You've done a good job at being shadows. Not good enough though."

She pressed a button on her mouse pad again. Yarrow, Vermilion, Zaffre and lots of other faces Grian didn't recognize filled the screens.

"The media found you guys too. They're going to run this today," Mushka continued. "They're linking the Council to the explosion in the Tipping Point and to you three kids. The line is the Council control the Proctors and you guys. You'll all be arrested on the spot if you're found."

Kids! Grian fumed. Mushka was hardly much older than them.

"Looks like I'm famous now too." Zaffre half smiled, biting his lower lip.

"That's why we came to you, Mushka," Jeffrey said. "You might be able to help us procure something from the Royal Science Museum. We are of the belief it will go some way to helping us save the sun."

"Procure?" The girl raised her eyebrows. "Don't you mean steal, Jef! What is this thing anyway?"

"It's a black mirror," Grian answered, as Zaffre took the folded leaflet from his pocket and handed it over.

"If you look up John Dee's exhibition at the Royal

Science Museum you should find information on his black mirror. That is what we are hoping to, ahem..."Jeffrey faltered.

"To nick!" Mushka winked before putting down the leaflet and pushing herself across to the other side of the room.

She stopped beside another cluster of screens on the right-hand wall and began typing into a keypad that popped out from the armrest of her chair. Lots and lots of information about John Dee and his Aztec black mirror began to populate the screens.

"And why will this mirror help save the sun?" she asked.

"We're not really sure," Grian replied, uncertain how much he should tell her. "The White Rose has written letters and we found one. It's written as a riddle and it seems to point to this black mirror."

Grian explained the riddle and how they'd figured out they were looking for the mirror, as Mushka typed on her keypad again and pulled up blueprint plans of the museum.

"Okay," she said, when he finished talking. "The John Dee exhibition is on the third floor of the Royal Science Museum. There's two access points, one at the front of the room and the other at the back. There's no direct exit from that floor to the outside, except through the windows, and I'm pretty sure no one wants to go that way. So you'd have to exit through either the front door or an emergency exit... Umm, could be tricky... Let me just take a quick look at their security detail..."

After two more minutes of tapping keys and flicking between screens, she said: "Great! It's not impossible, definitely doable... I could switch off cameras four, five and six, and maybe one of you could be a meat shield..."

Shelli raised her eyebrows. "Meat shield?"

"It's more Dungeons and Dragons talk – that's D&D for short," Jeffrey explained. "A meat shield is a player that can withstand a lot of damage and purposely blocks others from taking major damage, so that they can perform other tasks or duties during combat."

"Right..." Grian replied. "Bags not being the meat shield then."

Grian could hardly keep up as Mushka continued to spit out information about the museum and all the ways they could possibly access the mirror. Jeffrey looked in awe listening to her.

Eventually, after more searching online, black and white security camera footage appeared on Mushka's screen. The footage was of an empty street, an old-fashioned tram moving slowly along it.

"Is that a view from the front steps of the museum?" Zaffre leaned forward, astonished.

"I imagine that's precisely what it is," Jeffrey said, slapping his knee in excitement. "Mushka has just hacked their security system!"

"We can scope the place out and make a plan without stepping a foot inside," Mushka replied, her reaction much cooler than Jeffrey's. "Gives us better odds that you guys won't get caught."

The screen changed to what looked to be an internal view from high above an entrance door. Grian could see ticket scanners on the floor below.

"I'll make you IDs for those," Mushka said, opening a side screen to take notes. "This is already too easy!"

The camera angle shifted and they were now looking at a bright open space where a multi-storeyed staircase reached up to the top floor of the museum, which was covered in an ornate vaulted glass ceiling.

Mushka opened up the blueprint of the museum and highlighted the area they were looking at.

"These stairs will take you guys directly to the John Dee exhibition on the third floor. So, in the front door to the open plan stairwell, straight up those stairs and..."

The camera angle changed again. Now they were looking at a huge room. One wall of the room was covered from floor to ceiling in a graphic of a white bearded man wearing a black cap. The image of the man was superimposed over a backdrop of weird symbols like circles with crosses through their centre and strange swirly shapes. The words *Curiosity and investigation are central to our understanding of the universe today, as they were for John Dee...* were printed across the middle of the large-scale design.

"Looks like the right place," Mushka said, moving the camera around to look at the rest of the room.

Interactive screens, which were turned off for the night, were mixed side by side with big glass display cabinets filled with large and small oddities too detailed for Grian to see properly.

"Okay, where are you?" Mushka said, changing the screen to search the collections management system of the Science Museum. "Okay – great! The black mirror is item number thirteen in cabinet six... I'll just see if I can get a closer..."

The camera view switched again, to another corner of the room and then another.

"Aha, gotcha..." she mumbled, landing on a view she liked.

Mushka moved the camera around until it fell on a display cabinet where a shiny black disc sat in the centre, propped up on a clear plastic stand. The disc was about the size of a saucer that belonged to a tea set Grian's mam sometimes put out when they had guests.

On top of the display cabinet was an information card.

"Looks like we might have a match," Mushka said, zooming in enough to read the card.

John Dee's obsidian (volcanic glass) scrying mirror was originally used by Aztec high priests to conjure visions of the future and make prophecies. John Dee used his black mirror to carry out occult research into the world of spirits.

"It certainly seems you've found what we need," Jeffrey enthused, slapping Mushka firmly on the back.

As the girl almost choked, Grian noticed something small etched roughly into the bottom corner of the black mirror.

"Can you zoom in on that?" he asked, pointing at the screen.

"Let's see what these cameras can do," Mushka said, regaining her composure.

Mushka zoomed in so far the quality of the image became a little pixelated but even still he was sure he could make out the small etched letters on the disc.

"Is that *T.W.R?*" Zaffre gasped.

"The White Rose," Grian whispered in return. "So what do we do now?"

"Well – what you found me for…" Mushka smirked, looking back at the others. "We nick it!"

CHAPTER 28
DAYLIGHT ROBBERY

"My only worry really is the building does seem to have a pretty decent night-time alarm system and a lot of security guards on site, even at night," Mushka continued, moving the camera around so they could see a man with his feet up on a security desk as he played on his Hansom.. "So I think we make our move during the day. No one will expect it. I can disable the cameras and if we get the timings right, we could nick the mirror before anyone has a clue."

"Daylight robbery – that's quite genius!" Jeffrey gushed. "I would never have thought to steal anything during the day!"

"Probably because it's not a good idea," Grian replied. "We'll be seen."

"Not if we're quick," Mushka replied. "And the mirror is small, like it's definitely pocket sized."

"But how do we open the display cases?" Zaffre asked, rubbing his chin. "We can't break the glass. Surely that would be noticed!"

"By far the easiest way would be to get the master security card. See – it's kept here," she said, circling a room on the blueprint. "We'd need to get into that room somehow, which is a bit of a bummer since the door has an old-school locking system, i.e. it needs a metal key…"

"I have friends who hang out in museums and can easily slip right under any locked door," Shelli said quickly. "They'd steal a security card no hassle."

Mushka raised an eyebrow. "I want to meet these friends. They sound seriously cool!"

"I bet these friends are furry." Grian yawned, feeling suddenly very tired. "You probably wouldn't want to meet them in real life!"

"And when we do get this mirror…" Zaffre interrupted, slightly anxious. "Do you have any idea what we do with it?"

"We haven't in fact solved all the puzzle yet. Perhaps if we did, we may know what to do with the mirror once we procure it," Jeffrey stated. "I'm pretty satisfied we know what all the lines of the riddle refer to, except for the first and the last …"

"Only the Poet can see – that's the first line, isn't it?" Grian said, remembering. "But I can't remember the last one."

"In my heart the battle is won," Jeffrey answered.

"So de first and second lines are *Only de Poet can see, what's truly reflected in me?*" Shelli said, pacing the room now.

Nach began pacing too, feeding off her energy.

"Yes, exactamundo, Shelli." Jeffrey nodded awkwardly.

Grian cringed – Jeffrey never spoke like that. If he was trying to act cool in front of Mushka, it wasn't working.

"That mirror in de museum was used by de Aztecs to look into de future, wasn't it? Isn't that what you said scrying is, Zaffre?" Shelli asked.

"Yes, in a sense," the man agreed.

"So a bit like a Seer? De Wilde have Seers. They're sacred people, and they tell us our future."

Zaffre nodded "Yes. I have heard the Wilde have Seers. I would imagine scrying is just like that, except in scrying, the person telling your fortune uses an object, such as the black mirror, to do so."

"We have a famous Seer – Grian and Jeffrey met him when we were in de Forest of Coll. Amergin is his name."

"Just because he's a Seer doesn't mean he'll be able to help us, Shelli," Grian said, dismissing the idea.

"But let me finish, Grian. He's called de Poet – that's

de name he's known as in de Wilde. Amergin, de Poet. *Only de Poet can see, what's truly reflected in me.*"

"Seems pretty obvious to me," Mushka piped up from behind her computer. "Puzzle solved – that guy really needs to look in that mirror."

"Wow, that must be it!" Grian stood back, stunned. "But how could the White Rose know that Amergin is a Seer and that he's called the Poet, unless…"

"Unless the White Rose is Wilde too?" Jeffrey concluded.

"But who? How would someone from the Wilde know what Howard Hansom is up to? We hardly ever leave the forest," Shelli wondered.

A silence slipped through the group as everyone appeared to be lost in their own thoughts – except Mushka, who typed incessantly on her keypad.

Grian broke the silence, reciting the last line of the riddle: "*In my heart the battle is won.* What could that mean?"

"Oh!" Shelli gasped, jumping up excitedly. "I bet if de Poet looks into de heart of de black mirror, they'll see how to win de battle – how to save de sun."

"Yes. That's it!" Grian said, a rush of adrenaline flooding his tired body. "We've done it, we've solved the White Rose's riddle."

"All we have to do is break into the Royal Science

Museum and steal the black mirror." Jeffrey smiled, immediately dampening Grian's mood.

"I'll try get word to Mother now and ask her to get Amergin to meet us in de hForest outside of Hopper City – once we have de mirror. The hForest will be good cover, no one would ever think to look for de Wilde there."

For the next while they set about planning the break-in.

There was a vending machine downstairs in Giga Bite, and Mushka raided it, appearing with armfuls of junk food. It was really late and Grian hoped the sugar would help him stay awake, while keeping off the hunger.

"The café's my dad's place. He lets me hang out here when I'm staying with him." She shrugged, dumping the colourful plastic packets of sweets onto the floor. "Eat up!"

Grian's head buzzed with sugar. He stuffed his mouth full of jellies, trying hard to memorize the maps and video footage in preparation for their museum burglary the following morning.

Zaffre was the first one to nod off, his head slumping forward as his sat with his back to the wall. Then Shelli, who'd been using Nach as a pillow, began to snore. Exhausted, Grian told himself he was only closing his eyes for a minute, before drifting into a deep sleep.

*   *   *

When he woke, Grian wasn't sure what time it was. His neck was stiff and he winced trying to turn his head. Zaffre, Jeffrey and Mushka were all still asleep, but Nach and Shelli were gone.

He got up slowly and walked out onto the dark landing. The green neon lighting gave the place an eerie feel. At the bottom of the steps the outside door was open a crack, and a little of the dim morning light streamed inside.

He poked his head out into the fresh air. Shelli was sitting on an overturned crate to the side of the green door, Nach's head resting on her feet.

Grian stepped outside. Shelli smiled a little sadly up at him. She was playing with something in her hands. He sat down beside her and caught a glimpse of a small hairy grey mouse cupped inside her closed fist.

"Are you okay?" he asked.

"I'm fine," she said, shaking off her sadness.

"You can tell me," Grian encouraged.

"It's nothing really. I just see things sometimes, since Amergin touched my forehead in de forest. Things I don't always want to see, but...like I said, it's nothing," she answered, firmly closing down the topic.

"Oh," Grian replied, feeling uneasy. "Well if you ever want to talk..."

"De mice said they'll help us get de security card in de

museum," Shelli said, changing the subject. "I told them our plans. They're clever little things, so they should be fine."

"That's great," Grian said, "the plan's coming together."

Shelli looked weary as she put the tiny creature back down on the laneway and rubbed its head before the mouse scurried away. "De mouse said lots of her family are dying, Grian – already. She said it's because of what's happening to de sun – there's hardly any food growing and the days are colder. There isn't much time left for them..."

Grian looked up at the sky. The sun was just rising, the black mark like an angry bruise.

"I heard from Mother. Amergin had already contacted her – he must have had a vision. They've both set off for de hForest on de edge of Hopper City. They'll be there later tonight. We're to bring them de mirror."

"Soon, we'll be a step closer to saving it." Grian nodded at the sun.

Shelli didn't reply; she seemed to be deep in her thoughts. There were a few minutes of silence and Grian shifted awkwardly.

"I was thinking about what ya said last night, about de White Rose," she said, suddenly speaking up. "In de letter your grandad gave ya, it's obvious de White Rose knows

Adler – there was a line at de start saying their biggest mistake was leaving him. And ya said last night that ya thought de White Rose might be Wilde because, if we've read de riddle right, they know who Amergin is.

"I think ya might be right. Not many outside de Wilde know he's called de Poet. It got me thinking – did your granda know any Wilde people? I mean, like I told ya before, your name is Wilde and so is your sister's and mam's."

"I don't know." Grian shook his head. "But remember Mother knew who Grandad was? She told me that, the first night I met her in your forest."

"And she didn't like him much," Shelli added.

The main door opened and both looked up as Jeffrey stepped outside.

"Are you two alright out here? It's remarkably chilly for a summer's morning, especially as we're in Hopper. It's meant to be positively balmy here." He shivered, wrapping his arms around himself.

"Shelli thinks the White Rose could be Wilde too," Grian remarked, as Jeffrey sat down beside him.

"I was mulling over that very idea myself last night. It occurred to me the White Rose has to be someone close to Hansom, otherwise how would they know what he's up to. Then I remembered the article in *The Techie* – *Edition 542*, where Hansom spoke about his Wilde roots.

Don't you remember, he told us about it himself in the Tipping Point. His mother was Wilde and she left the community when she met his father."

"Do you think his *mother* could be the White Rose?" Grian asked.

"Not in the slightest," Jeffrey confirmed. "I've seen interviews with her. She's quite a callous creature and hopelessly devoted to her son. I can't see it, if I'm honest. But maybe she's still in touch with some people from the Wilde and has spilled her son's secrets?"

"I'll ask Mother about her when we meet with Amergin. She might be able to tell us more," Shelli said, just as Zaffre poked his head out the door.

"We were wondering where you three had gotten to... Come on, it's almost time!"

CHAPTER 29

THE BELLE SISTERS

"We need to get moving soon," Zaffre announced, munching his way through one of the packets of crisps Mushka had given them for breakfast.

Mushka was staring at the blueprint of the museum again, mumbling something under her breath while flipping back and forth through different camera angles.

"Right, the night shift are almost done. The new shift starts in one hour at nine. I want you guys entering the premises at changeover just when the museum opens for the day. The security detail will be talking to each other and catching up on the night – they'll be off guard."

"Off guard, that's very humorous," Jeffrey gushed.

Mushka grimaced and shook her head.

"I configured these," she said, ignoring Jeffrey while she pulled out watches and EarPods from a desk drawer. "They're preloaded with museum tickets and a fake digital ID for each of you. They may look like Hansom devices, but that's just a dummy case. They are my own inventions and untraceable."

"Genius," Jeffrey gushed once more. "May I never take it off!"

"Oh, Mushka, I love you," Grian teasingly whispered to Jeffrey, as he picked up his own device.

Jeffrey smiled, not looking even the slightest bit embarrassed.

"I've a watch for you too, Zaffre," Mushka said, handing over a fourth device.

Zaffre shuddered a little taking the watch from Mushka. "I find these a little repulsive nowadays," he commented, as he put it on.

Grian felt weird wearing a watch and EarPods again. He tightened the strap and tried to shake off his nervous energy. Shelli was completely awkward wearing her watch, even holding her wrist at a weird angle so it almost looked broken.

"Just pretend it's not there," Grian told her. "After a while you won't notice it."

"Won't notice it!" Shelli groaned. "I can feel de thing pulsing, like it's alive. It's tingling my wrist. And these

236

pods feel terrible in my ears – like I've stuffed them full of chewing gum."

"Well, you'll just have to get used to it I'm afraid, Shelli," Jeffrey replied. "Otherwise you'll stand out, and the prime objective of any good thief is to fit in. Also, good communication is a vital part of any plan."

"Make sure your EarPods are switched on too – I will be talking to you through them. Otherwise it'll be a TPK," Mushka warned, showing Shelli how to use hers.

"Total party kill – right you are." Jeffrey nodded.

Grian wished he knew more about "Dungeons and Dragons". He was finding what Mushka said almost as difficult to follow sometimes as Jeffrey.

"Now that we're all ready, I'll go home and wait for Yarrow and the others. If they are not there, I'll get word out to the Council, let them know what's happening. All going to plan, we'll meet you in the hForest. I'll keep Mushka up to date," Zaffre said, heading for the door.

Though it was after eight, the morning was still half dark as they stepped outside. The threesome said goodbye to Zaffre in the alleyway and then waited for a short while, testing to make sure the EarPods and watches worked at a distance before saying goodbye to Mushka. Grian got lost in memorizing their plans as his new watch guided him towards the museum – he'd fallen back into the old habit of relying on it very quickly.

They walked past shops that were just readying to open their doors, and cafés where the early morning crowd queued for their coffees, before they stopped outside the museum Grian had only ever seen virtually up to now.

The tram passed by behind him, its old-fashioned bell ringing through the busy morning street. He watched Shelli go through the entrance, then Jeffrey, until it was his turn. He pulled his hat down securely on his head and climbed the steps.

The security guard just inside the door looked a little harassed and was busy checking for something in his pockets. Grian held his breath and swiped his fake Hansom over the entrance barrier. It beeped before zipping open. He tried not to look relieved as he slipped inside.

His hands were shaking, so he shoved them firmly into his pockets and pretended to look at some of the displays while casually making his way towards the stairs.

As planned, Shelli was the first to climb the ornate wooden steps straight in front of them. She was headed for the staffroom, where the master security card was kept.

Jeffrey went up next, heading straight for the John Dee exhibition, where it was his job to locate the mirror. While he hung around, he would also take notes and pictures with his watch, so if anyone asked he could say he was preparing a school project.

Grian was the last to go upstairs. His job was to distract any security guard who might happen to head Shelli's way while she waited for her mice to steal the master security card from the staffroom.

The staffroom was located three quarters of the way along a dark, mahogany-panelled hall near the top of the stairs.

Grian took position at one end of the hall and peered round the corner, spotting Shelli kneeling on the floor outside the staffroom. A small mouse sat on her palm, looking up at her as if listening to instructions. Then Shelli bent forward and kissed the mouse on the nose, before it jumped off her palm and scuttled under the door.

The museum was quiet; so quiet the echo of a guard coughing downstairs filled the space.

A while passed and Shelli still hadn't shown up with the master card. Grian peered back round the corner nervously. Shelli was still on her knees, her left ear to the floor, she was trying to look under the door. There was no sign of the mouse.

"*Security guard alert,*" Mushka's voice suddenly sounded through Grian's EarPods.

Quickly, Shelli stood up and pretended to inspect a painting in the hall. Grian turned around just in time to see a large man in a white shirt mounting the top step of the stairs.

"Good morning," Grian said as the guard passed on his rounds.

He kicked himself when the guard disappeared round a corner ahead. He was trying so hard to appear normal that he was beginning to act a little like Jeffrey and not normal at all.

When he was sure the man had gone, Grian slipped down the hallway towards Shelli. Something had to be up, she was taking too long.

"What's going on?" he hissed. "We need to get moving."

"She's stuck," Shelli replied, her amber eyes wide with fright as she bent down on to her knees again.

Grian could see the thin tail and grey furry bottom of the tiny mouse shimmying from side to side as it poked out from under the door. The animal was straining to pull something with it.

"The card's wedged stuck," Shelli said, panicking.

Grian poked his finger under the door gap and tried to flick at the silver keyring attached to the card. The ring appeared a little too large to slip under and seemed to be what was causing the jam. Flicking at it wasn't working – the card was still stuck.

"*Do we need to abort the mission?*" Mushka asked over the airways.

"No," Grian replied, shaking his head. "We just need some time. We'll figure it out."

He steadied his breath, stood up and left the corridor, heading for the nearest exhibition. He stopped by one of the glass display cabinets. Pretending to be interested in its contents, he waited for his mind to stop racing. After a few minutes, both Shelli and Jeffrey joined him.

"Apart from getting the key, there's no other way to open that staffroom door," Jeffrey stuttered, when they were all together. "It's old-school technology...unless we shoulder-barge it but I'm afraid that would cause quite a stir!"

"What about the mouse, Shelli? Isn't there anything she can do? Maybe she can find another way out?" Grian replied, frustrated.

"I've sent her back in to look," Shelli confirmed, "but she hasn't found anything yet."

The large security guard passed them again. Grian moved away from his friends, so as not to raise suspicion. He sat down on a bench in front of a painting of a starry night.

"How do you unlock an old-fashioned door without a key," he whispered into his watch.

An hTube video began playing on the small screen. The video was of a man opening a locked door using various items. First the man used a hairclip, but Grian didn't know where he'd get one of those, then he used a drill and then a credit card.

"That's it – a card!" Grian said, trying to stay composed. He spoke slowly into his watch to his friends. "Has anyone got a card, like a thick plastic one?"

"I've the library sign-up card I picked up in Dunstan," Jeffrey replied, pulling the folded leaflet from his pocket.

Jeffrey separated the plastic card from the leaflet and headed across the room. Grian grabbed the card and walked calmly back to the staffroom door. Shelli followed quickly behind.

"You better be fast," Mushka whispered, *"I'm moving the security cameras more than I would like. I don't want anyone to suss it."*

Grian played the video again and followed the instructions. He steadied his shaking hand before slipping the card in between the doorframe and the door. He nudged the card downwards until he felt the lock. He pushed hard, but unlike in the video the lock didn't give. He tried again, but the resistance was too solid to break.

"Hurry," Mushka encouraged him.

Grian's heart thumped and his hand was shaking badly now. He closed his eyes and roared at himself inside his head that he could do it!

This time he moved the card down much faster. When he felt the pressure, he shimmied the card into position between the lock and the frame. Then he pushed hard until he felt the click. His heart skipped.

Quickly he turned the lock, and the door opened.

"We're in!" He strained not to shout the words out in excitement.

Shelli grabbed the mouse and master security card from the floor. Grian shut the door and the pair walked as naturally as possible back towards the exhibition.

His heart was still pounding when he stopped at the entrance to the John Dee exhibition. The place was quiet. He pretended to look at the welcome video while Shelli approach the glass cabinet that held the mirror.

He watched out the side of his eye as she quickly glanced around before swiping the security card over the black box that controlled the locking system. Grian barely noticed her hand swoop in and snatch the shiny black disc from its stand.

He stiffened, wondering if an alarm would sound but none did. Shelli quickly placed the mirror into the waistband of her trousers before walking away. Within seconds, she was out of the exhibition room and down the stairs.

"*You go, girl!*" Mushka whooped into his ear.

Grian grimaced and turned down the volume of his EarPods. They had decided to leave one at a time so as not to look suspicious. So with what he hoped was an air of calm, he strolled through the exhibition, browsing displays as though he hadn't a care.

Jeffrey headed down the steps next. He was taking his time too, and right now looked very convincing as he pretended to be fascinated by a broken jug displayed on the wall.

Grian had wandered out of the John Dee exhibition and into another room where a small carousel sat in the middle of the large open space. The exhibit here seemed to be on the history of the circus in Babbage.

He was just strolling past mounted images on the wall when a black and white photo grabbed his attention.

The photo was filled with a cast of strange characters lined up outside a high-top tent. A giant hairy man held a monkey in his arms standing beside a woman who wore a headdress of feathers and not much else. Two men in top hats and tails stood in the middle of the image, and on the edges of the frame were a host of animals, including a tiger and two enormous elephants.

Sitting on the ground at the front, staring straight at the camera, were three grubby young white-haired girls. The girl sat centre of the threesome looked a little older than the other two, and had her arms protectively round their shoulders. There was something familiar in her determined stare.

An information card under the image read: *This is one*

of the last photos of the Belle Sisters, from the famous travelling circus The Barnaby Brothers. The sisters disappeared shortly after this was taken.

Grian wasn't sure why the hair on his arms stood up, as he took a picture of the photo with his watch.

"*Grian, what are you doing? You need to leave now. Jeffrey has just exited,*" Mushka said, pulling him from his thoughts. "*You need to get out, there's...*"

The line went dead. Grian removed his EarPods and shook them before putting them back in, but nothing happened. He couldn't hear Mushka.

Grian was on edge heading down the stairs. As he got closer to the open entrance door ahead, he could see the cars and trams passing by on the street outside. As he got closer again, he could see Shelli at the bottom of the museum steps talking to two men.

The men looked like his dad and Vermilion. But what were they doing here?

"Hey, stop!" someone called behind him.

His blood chilled. He kept walking, acting as if he hadn't heard a thing. Just a few more steps and he would be outside too.

"Hey, you – stop!" the person said again.

Grian was sweating and his breath was heavy now, but he kept walking. He was almost at the exit.

Someone grabbed his shoulder. Grian turned round

and quickly pressed his EarPods, pretending he'd been listening to something on them. He was looking straight at the wide chest of the security guard that had passed him earlier.

"You dropped this." The guard scowled handed over Jeffrey's blank library card.

"Ahem...thanks!" Grian tried to hide the shake in his hand reaching for the object.

The security guard looked suspicious and was about to say something, when a shrill cry cut the air.

"Help! Someone, help! It's them! It's them," a woman screamed on the street outside.

CHAPTER 30

THE DOUBLE CROSS

"You stay put here – I want to talk to you," the security guard warned Grian, as he moved away past him to check on the commotion outside.

Grian waited until the security guard was distracted outside, then snuck out behind him.

He was looking around for his friends from the top step, when he stumbled back in fright. At the bottom of the steps five Proctors hovered in a circle around Shelli, Vermilion and his dad.

He watched in horror as some of the Proctors threw their hands out and his dad, Shelli and Vermilion stiffened like planks of wood and hovered up into the air. Nach was howling frantically, pulling at one of the Proctor's cloaks, when another in the cloaked group flung their arm wide. Nach yelped and flew backwards and smacked against a street light.

"Stop!" the security guard roared, racing down the steps while pulling out a taser gun.

Another Proctor turned swiftly, and a wave of air hit the security guard straight in the stomach, somersaulting him backwards against the stone wall of the museum.

"No, no! Dad!" Grian cried, sprinting down the steps.

A black truck hovered waiting on the street and Grian watched his dad and the others being bundled inside before the truck moved away without a sound. Some people on the pavements stood stunned, while others screamed and shouted into their Hansoms for help or rushed to help the fallen security guard.

"Psst! Over here, Grian," Jeffrey called, peeking out from behind a bench at the bottom of the steps.

"Jeffrey! What happened? What's...what's going on?" Grian stuttered.

"*Guy...guys, can anyone hear me? Your watches went dead. Hello...hello?*" Mushka's anxious voice suddenly sounded in their ears.

"My dad, Shelli, Ver... They're gone... They've been kidnapped by the Proctors," Grian told her, trembling. "What were Dad and Vermilion doing here anyway?"

"*I was trying to tell you guys the two of them were on their* way to meet you, but the signals went down," Mushka explained. "Zaffre told me Vermilion, your dad and Yarrow were waiting at his house when he got home. Zaffre told them the plan – he, Yarrow and Vermilion were going to go straight to the hForest and your dad was coming here to see you were okay – but Vermilion insisted he join your dad. He said he was worried about you."

"The Proctors must have blocked the signals. But how did they know we were here?" Grian asked, anxiously voicing the questions in his head. "Could someone have been tracking our watches? Were they tracking Dad and Vermilion somehow? Why only take the two of them and Shelli though – it doesn't make sense?"

"Those watches are not trackable," Mushka replied, sounding puzzled too. "Someone could have spotted Vermilion or you three and reported it? I know you were careful, but your faces are everywhere. And maybe the Proctors got spooked when you didn't come out together, and didn't have time to wait for you two so just took the others?"

"Or maybe they somehow knew Shelli was carrying the mirror – and that's what they're truly after!?" Jeffrey exclaimed. "Now Hansom will get his hands on it."

"We need to follow them!" Grian said quickly. "They're in one of Hansom's blacked-out hHover trucks. Can you track it somehow, Mushka?"

"I'll find the truck on street cameras and track it that way,

then I can direct you guys..." Mushka announced. *"Hold on...
What – what's going on? This has never happened before. The
cameras are going out all over the city – all electronic
equipment is failing... I can't track them!"*

Grian looked around panicked, unable to think straight,
when he felt a slight pull on the back of his trousers.

"Nach!" he gasped, turning swiftly around.

The small fox had the leg of his trousers in her teeth
and was pulling hard and growling.

"Okay – take us to Shelli, girl!" Grian said, feeling the
fox wanted them to follow her.

Quickly, the animal turned and darted off down the
street. Grian and Jeffrey raced after her. The pair were
both struggling for air by the time they reached a set of
traffic lights on the outskirts of Hopper City.

The lights marked the entrance to an industrial estate
and Nach dashed straight in.

*"Guys, you are killing it – serious athletic vibes! You're in
Corporate Creek Business Park,"* Mushka told them, *"but
what would the Proctors be doing there?"*

Grian and Jeffrey followed Nach past several dull grey
buildings. All of the buildings were square, with flat roofs
and hardly any windows. They lined both sides of the
quiet estate road.

Nach stopped outside one of the larger premises and
began to whimper.

"They must be in there," Grian whispered, ducking down behind a low wall that surrounded the place.

He peered over the wall. The building was on a corner site. Its front facade had more glass than most of the others around but unusually the glass was black, so it was impossible to see through.

Grian snapped a picture on his watch and sent it to Mushka.

"Can you tell us anything about this place?" he whispered.

Mushka sounded unsettled. *"That building appears to have been the old postal sorting office for the Hopper district, but it was closed down a few years ago."*

"It was a sorting office?" Grian gulped.

"Just like the warehouse in the Tipping Point," Jeffrey whispered.

The pair decided to slip along by the wall, around the back, for a look.

Grian bristled when he saw the black hHover truck parked in a small car park around the back of the building. There were no windows on this side of the building but there was a large roller door in the corrugated grey exterior, which was partly opened.

"Stay here, girl," Grian ordered Nach.

He beckoned Jeffrey to follow him, then snuck forward and took a peek before shimmying under the door.

The warehouse was dark inside. The only light came from dirty plastic roof tiles above and the slightly opened roller door. Across a patch of concrete flooring from them were rows and rows of shelving. The shelves were stacked high in crates, just like the ones loaded on the truck in Dunstan.

The boys crept forwards into one of the aisles and Grian picked out a small yellow crystal from a crate on the shelf beside him.

"That is surely what they are mining in Dunstan," Jeffrey gasped. "There must be thousands upon thousands of crystals here…"

Then Grian noticed all the crates on one side of the aisle were marked *Phase Two*, while on the other side, some were labelled *Phase Three and others Phase Four*.

"What does 'Phase Three' and 'Phase Four' mean?" he whispered. The wording niggled at a memory.

Something clattered nearby and the lights came on. Grian and Jeffrey ducked down, squeezing between stacks of crates on the bottom shelf.

From this vantage point, Grian could see a large trapdoor in the concrete floor near the roller door, which he hadn't noticed in the darkness. It opened, gradually revealing steps down into the ground under the warehouse.

The pair ducked further into hiding when three men

and two women in long dark cloaks floated up through the open trapdoor into the room. Then, without a word, the hoodless Proctors flicked their wrists and began moving crates from the shelves without touching them, just like they had done in Dunstan. Carefully, each Proctor hovered close to their own stack, guiding it through the warehouse and down the steps back underground.

"We need to follow them," Grian whispered, as the last Proctor disappeared back down through the trapdoor.

He was about to move when another man hurried up the steps into the warehouse. This man carried a backpack and was wearing a hoody. He wore his sun-streaked, wavy, brown hair tied back in a ponytail, and his sallow face was pale, strained and lined in worry. Even so, he looked very well for someone presumed by the world to be dead.

Grian's stomach churned. He felt physically sick.

"Howard Hansom!" Jeffrey mouthed, his eyes almost popping from his face.

"Be quick with those second phase crates. Leave the others – we can come back for them. Time is ticking," Hansom ordered a Proctor who'd floated back up the stairs behind him. "The Loop needs to leave in a half hour if we're to make the morning schedule."

"The Hyperloop?" Jeffrey whispered. "But I thought it only travelled from Turing to the Tipping Point!"

"When we found Solas in the Tipping Point, she said the volunteers thought Hansom was building another Hyperloop line, remember – maybe he built it to Hopper?" Grian hissed quietly.

Suddenly a loud clatter sounded from the other side of the warehouse behind them.

"What is he doing now?! He knows we need to leave soon," Hansom muttered, as he strode along one of the shelving aisles and through a set of double doors.

"Come on." Grian kept low and crawled quickly after the man.

Jeffrey hesitated for a moment before following behind.

Grian stopped at the double doors and eased the left one open. He snuck through, his heart pounding, and held the door for Jeffrey.

This side of the warehouse was full of luggage and removals boxes. Grian and Jeffrey crawled across the cold cement floor and hid behind a huge pile of suitcases.

The suitcases had name tags and some even had coloured ribbons wrapped around their handles – a trick Grian's mam sometimes used to distinguish their stuff. The removals boxes were all labelled too.

A cardboard box beside Grian was half open. Inside was a mix of sports equipment, teddy bears and clothes. A sticker on the box read *Peter, Patricia, Philip and Susie Peters*, and the address said *Their new home, the Tipping*

Point. The large box was decorated in the hand-drawn love hearts of a young child.

Grian trembled. He remembered the adverts where the smiling drivers of Hansom's removals company waved at roadside well-wishers while supposedly relocating people's luggage to the Tipping Point. Like everything else, those adverts were lies – this must be where Hansom dumped the volunteers' belongings.

Then he remembered all the excited volunteers telling their stories on the screen walls of the Tipping Point's main Hyperloop station. The Peters family had to be one of those stories. He tried not to think about what had happened to the Peters or to all the other families whose name tags hung from the suitcases around them.

"How did you lose the boys?" Hansom snapped from somewhere across the large space.

"I thought they'd be with the girl, but they weren't," a different man replied. "And the mirror was my priority. I didn't have time to wait for them too."

A chill raced down Grian's spine; he was sure he knew this other voice. He peered out but couldn't see the men.

"But you said you overheard that Slight boy in Dunstan saying something about Adler's secret letter. I need that letter, and they need to be stopped! Having the whole world looking for them doesn't seem to be enough of a deterrent."

So Grian *had* seen a shadow outside their door in Dunstan just before they went to sleep.

"I overheard the children say something about having another letter, but neither Yarrow, Zaffre or that idiot postman seemed to know anything about it. Children are delusional, Howard, they make things up all the time. I wouldn't worry about them! That postman, Cam, said Adler told him the White Rose sent three letters in total not four. You already have one of those letters – and no one knows that. And now you have this black mirror – a result of a second letter. If Cam is right that means there is only one letter left to find. And whether the children have another one or not is irrelevant, as whatever the White Rose was planning surely can't work now."

"Maybe. But the letter I found led me to Adler, who still won't speak. And the riddle in that letter also points to two other people, two other people who are clearly important and I haven't figured out who they are, so essentially I have nothing except this mirror and a stubborn old man. We don't know anything about the White Rose's plan or how it might potentially stop me stealing the sun.

"We need to find the last letter and find out if those children have a secret letter or not! We've worked too hard and too long for this. Things are getting very close, we're almost there. We cannot afford for anything to go wrong, so we need to worry about everything right now, including those darned children. Kids or not, they must be stopped!"

Grian couldn't believe what he'd just heard. Howard Hansom was stealing the sun. He had said so himself. But why, and how? And Grandad was still alive! And he clearly hadn't told Hansom anything about the secret letter or the crystal the White Rose sent him.

Quickly and quietly he followed the voices and crawled behind another pile of suitcases. Peering over the top, he could see two men shadowed in the near distance.

Hansom's hands were on his hips. He was glaring at the second man, who was pacing up and down in front of him. Grian was sure now he knew the other man – he'd been pacing the first time Grian had seen him too, in the abandoned underground postal station, his long coat whipping at his ankles every time he turned.

"Vermilion," he whispered, his thoughts racing.

He never really liked him, but he had believed Vermilion was on their side. He had believed he was a Council member working undercover for Hansom in order to find out his plans. Even Yarrow had told Grian he could trust him. But now it appeared Vermilion was truly working for Hansom and double-crossing them all.

CHAPTER 31

THE HYPERLOOP

"But if I destroy the black mirror," Vermilion said, holding it up, "surely, the rest of this White Rose's plan falls apart. And you can get on with what you're meant to be doing."

"Give the mirror to me!" Hansom directed.

Vermilion hesitated. "No. I'll take it for you – you've too much on your plate."

"I said give it to me," Hansom snarled.

Vermilion hesitated before slowly passing it over. Hansom looked at the black mirror for a moment then placed it into the *PEOPLEPOWER* backpack he was carrying. He put the bag back on his shoulders without fully closing it.

"I can hear a mumbled version through your EarPods, but

can you record this, guys, so I can get a closer look? This is some serious BBEG stuff," Mushka whispered.

Jeffrey angled his wrist and set record on his watch.

"I might destroy the mirror when I get back," Hansom told Vermilion. "I want to have a closer look at it first – I feel a plan forming. But I still need the White Rose's remaining letters! This will go down as the biggest achievement in history. I am a real-life Noah, and I will do whatever necessary to secure my ark. While the rest of the planet and everyone on it slips mindlessly towards death, I am the only one clever and brave enough to cut the fodder and save the cream of the crop, the elites of humanity.

"I am moulding a future where human life won't just go on for millennia but, without bloodlines corrupted by the ignorant masses, it will thrive! It is vital we make sure there are no loose ends, or the earthquake and the Tipping Point and PEOPLEPOWER and all our work will have been for nothing; we will never steal the sun and everything we've been planning for years, not to mention our very existence as a species, will be destroyed."

Grian shivered, petrified, as Hansom fumed.

"Woah... Did he, like, just call almost the whole world 'the ignorant masses'?" Mushka whispered incredulously down their EarPods. *"That is some mega twisted stuff he's spewing."*

"You're sounding paranoid now, Howard," Vermilion replied. "You need to calm down. Leave finding the letter or letters to me! I can firmly put an end to the White Rose's plans. You just concentrate on what you're meant to be doing. Otherwise everything we've been working for will be destroyed, but it won't be because of some blasted White Rose! Now, the Hyperloop is going soon. Are you taking those two with you?"

Vermilion turned and pointed. Grian gripped Jeffrey's arm, horrified. For the first time he noticed two figures floating silently a little off the floor in a dark corner behind Vermilion. Shelli and his dad stared straight ahead unblinking, their arms pinned to their sides. A Proctor stood by them, subtly moving his gloved hand like a puppet master, controlling the pair.

"Just be careful how you speak to me. No one, brother or not, has a guaranteed place," Hansom replied, shaking a finger at Vermilion. "You get back in touch with the Council. Tell Yarrow you got away from the Proctors. They may start to distrust you, but play along for a while yet. I'll see what the Wilde girl and the postman have to say for themselves when we get back. They might not be as tough as old Adler."

"Noted, brother." Vermilion snorted, swooping around in his long black coat and striding by the suitcases out through the double doors.

"Brother?" Jeffrey mouthed, as the pair ducked down.

"Get those two to the Loop. If everything's loaded, it's

time to go," Hansom ordered the Proctor, before also passing close by the two boys back the way he came.

Grian shivered, watching the Proctor flick his wrist so that Shelli and his dad moved out of the corner and hovered through the double doors and into the other side of the warehouse. He felt sick. He couldn't let Hansom take them away on the Loop, just like he had his grandad.

"Vermilion is working with Hansom, and Hansom called him brother?! And he must have heard me say something about your grandad's letter when we were in Dunstan!" Jeffrey blurted, as if dying to get the words out. "But he's on the Council – Yarrow trusts Ver—"

"And Hansom is somehow saving his rich and powerful friends – I'm guessing that's what he meant when he said elites – by stealing the sun and leaving the rest of us and the planet to die!?" Mushka whispered urgently. "And, what is this about a secret letter, do you guys have one?"

"Yes we do," Grian divulged. Mushka had heard Vermilion. He had to tell her. "I promise I will tell you about it later. But you cannot tell anyone, no one except Yarrow knows. But right now we have to get Dad, Shelli and the mirror."

The line was silent for a minute before Mushka spoke again.

"Okay I can wait. If you guys trust me, then I guess I can trust you too."

"You're a valued part of this team now Mushka," Jeffrey added.

"Less of the team bit, Jef," she answered.

The pair crept back through the swing doors and between the shelving units in time to catch Hansom, the Proctor, Grian's dad and Shelli disappearing down the steps underground.

Grian raced for the trapdoor in the floor, Jeffrey just behind him.

He snuck down the steps a safe distance from the Proctor. The cold air licked his skin. He could see a concrete platform ahead. He took another step down and the ultra-sleek, bullet-like, bright white Hyperloop came into view. His breath caught, like it had the first time he'd seen the Loop, when he was waiting to board it to the Tipping Point. Now, instead of excited people occupying the neon blue *PEOPLEPOWER* branded seats, they were stacked full of crates.

Grian stopped and pulled in beside the wall of the steps just out of view. Howard Hansom was speaking to one of the Proctors on the platform.

"What are we going to do? How are we going to stop them?" Grian's voice trembled as nervous energy washed through him.

"What are you seeing, guys?" Mushka spoke up.

"The Hyperloop is on tracks a few metres in front and

to the left of our position," Jeffrey whispered into his watch. "The Proctors are just finishing loading it with crates of the yellow crystals. Then it appears they will load up Grian's dad and Shelli."

"*Doesn't the Hyperloop use magnetic levitation?*" Mushka asked quickly.

"Yes…that is correct." Jeffrey's reply was slow, as if forming a thought.

"*Well, what if we could stop it by disrupting the magnetic field with—*" Mushka continued.

"A pulse train," Jeffrey interrupted excitedly.

"*Exactly, Jef!*" Mushka replied.

"What's a pulse train?" Grian whispered.

"An EMP – an electromagnetic pulse," Jeffrey answered. "An EMP can disrupt other magnetic fields. Examples of EMPs are lightning strikes or a meteor hit…"

"Well, we can't exactly make that happen," Grian replied, panicking a little.

"*No, but we could cause a power surge,*" Mushka announced.

"Genius!" Jeffrey whispered. "Do you have access to the power grid?"

The girl laughed. "*Do you even need to ask!*"

"Whatever you're doing, you better do it fast," Grian hissed.

Hansom was walking towards the Hyperloop, the

PEOPLEPOWER backpack strapped to his back.

"*Get ready,*" Mushka replied. "*Once I cause the surge, you need to run, grab your dad, Shelli and the mirror and get out of there fast!*"

Grian was about to reply when suddenly sparks flew through the air and there were bangs and booms from everything electrical in sight. Shrieks of panic washed through the space as the Hyperloop dropped from the air and crashed onto the rails below, its doors opening and closing rapidly of their own accord.

A power line that ran down the centre of the tunnel ceiling fizzed and sizzled until there was a huge pop and the wire broke free from its hold to dance around the air, twisting and turning like a vicious and frenzied snake biting at everything in sight.

Grian's dad and Shelli collapsed onto the concrete platform, when the Proctor who'd been controlling them lapsed in concentration because the fluorescent lights above had burst into smithereens.

The place was plunged into darkness, except for the sparks that flew from the live wire dancing dangerously through the space.

Grian raced from hiding.

"You get Dad and Shelli," he shouted at Jeffrey, who scrambled out behind him. "I'll get the mirror."

Howard Hansom had his back to him and was shouting

at the Proctors when Grian reached for the backpack and pulled it off the man's shoulder.

Hansom spun around.

"You! What do you think you're doing?" he roared, his eyes flashing in recognition.

He grabbed a strap of the backpack and yanked it back.

Grian gritted his teeth and held on. The strap snapped under pressure and the mirror flew out from inside it and clattered over the edge of the platform onto the tracks behind the train.

Grian could hardly catch his breath. Without thinking, he jumped down onto the tracks and fumbled around in the darkness. It was impossible to spot the mirror in the tunnel, which was pitch black except for the intermittent flashing of light from the live wire.

"You stupid fool!" Hansom spat from the platform above. "You've lost the mirror! You really are the boy everybody loves to hate!"

"The world will hate you when they find out what you're up to! You're stealing the sun for some sick reason and letting us all die!" Grian shook, screaming the words with a depth of anger he didn't know he had.

"By the time the world finds out what's happening, it'll be too late," Hansom sneered.

"You live here too!" Grian cried, a vicious rage ripping through him. "Why would you steal the sun and kill

265

everything? What do you think you're doing? How can you believe you're saving anyone if the world is dying?!"

"Come with me and I'll show you what I'm doing, Grian." Hansom smiled calmly.

The outline of a Proctor appeared silently beside him on the platform.

The Proctor extended their gloved hand, then made a fist. Grian yelped and squirmed, suddenly choking. It felt like the Proctor was right beside him on the track, squeezing all the air from his neck. The more he wriggled the tighter their grip grew, until the corners of his vision began to blur. He couldn't breathe.

In his mind he saw the hazy outline of his grandad in the Tipping Point warehouse. Grian had let him down. He was useless. Hansom was right: Grian was the boy everyone should hate. He'd let everyone down. He was never going to save the world.

Then a piercing cry ripped through the tunnel, echoing off the round walls. Grian collapsed onto the tracks. The grip on his neck released and he spluttered, gasping for air. For a minute he thought he had made the terrifying sound himself, until the Proctor tumbled down onto the track beside him, engulfed by a sea of cackling birds that continued to fly torpedo-like down the steps from the warehouse above.

Dazed, Grian started crawling away. The tunnel filled

with a terrifying choir of human and animal cries as the frenzy of birds armed with razor-sharp beaks attacked Hansom and the Proctors.

"Come on!" Shelli was beside him, pulling him to his feet.

Jeffrey and his dad were there now too. They helped him quickly along the tracks, away from the scene.

"The mirror – I don't have the mirror," he stuttered, hesitating.

"It doesn't matter! We have to get out of here! This way," his dad insisted, pulling him away.

The cries and screams dulled a little the further they travelled, until they came to a dead end.

"There's nowhere to go," Grian's dad panicked. "I thought this was the old postal railway line – it should have led us back to Hopper's main post office. I don't understand!"

Quickly, Shelli took her Glimmer from her backpack and lit it up. The soft light fell on the cement wall straight in front of them. While the others looked around for any way to escape, Grian was stuck deep in thought, longing to go back.

He'd lost the mirror. Hansom would probably find it once the birds had gone. They would never save the sun now.

A noise startled him in the darkness and Nach bounded forward into the dim light.

The fox held something in her mouth and she dropped it at his feet.

"Nach, you've found the mirror," he gasped, relieved, falling to his knees to hug the fox.

CHAPTER 32
VIRAL

"In the Tipping Point, Hansom built his Hyperloop line parallel to the old postal underground railway line," Jeffrey mused moving along the tunnel wall, back the way they had come. "We accessed the postal line via a door in the wall. What if it's the same here in Hopper? Maybe there is a door into the postal railway line somewhere along here, just like there was in the Tipping Point..."

The others followed him, frantically searching the curved walls. The sounds of the birds and the Proctors' cries grew eerily close again.

"Yes! Here." Shelli's voice broke through the commotion.

She stood by a circular iron door in the wall with a

metal steering-wheel-like handle. She was straining to turn the handle when Grian and his dad raced up to help. After a few seconds the stiff handle gave way and they twisted the metal wheel round until the door creaked open. Grian's dad was the first to climb through.

"You're right, Jeffrey," he exclaimed, standing on the other side of the round opening. "This is the old Hopper postal tunnel! It makes sense now. The postal railway tunnels wouldn't be large enough to fit the Hyperloop, so Hansom made his own tunnels."

The others climbed in to join his dad, and when it was Grian's turn he felt he'd stepped into a memory.

The cement ceiling of the Hopper railway tunnel, just like the one in the Tipping Point, was low and curved. A row of cobwebbed industrial strip lights ran along its centre like a spine, and rusted railways tracks lined the dirt floor.

"*G, disconnect your EarPods so your dad can hear me too,*" Mushka said.

Grian did as he was told, and Mushka's voice came out directly from his watch to fill the tunnel.

"*I'll find a map of the railway tunnel on the hNet, Mr Woods. It might help you guys find a way out.*"

"No need. I studied these postal lines for years," his dad shouted, louder than was necessary. "They've always fascinated me…"

"Where does this tunnel lead to, Dad?" Grian asked.

"It's the Hopper district line. It goes from the main Hopper City post office the whole way to Babbage Central Sorting Warehouse, Grian, which was located under the Tipping Point. It linked up to the Quantum postal line there too, but the Quantum line began to collapse in a few places years ago, even before the earthquake, because of mining around the city. It was never fixed and that line was eventually shut down. When the postal service started to become somewhat obsolete, the whole postal underground railway was shut – it was a sad day for all postal workers. Anyway, if I am right, then I think I know where we can escape above ground. If we go this way, we will head straight under the Hopper City post office. It's one of our most active offices, wait until you see!"

"Make haste, Mr Woods," Jeffrey said, hurrying them along. "I'm somewhat nervous about what might happen should Hansom come after us."

"Don't worry, Jeffrey – he'll be stuck for a while with my feathered friends." Shelli smiled.

"*And when the BBEG does manage to surface,*" Mushka said over the airwaves, "*Hansom is in for a big surprise!*"

"What might that be?" Jeffrey asked, curious.

Mushka laughed. "*Let's just say the hNet loves him right now.*"

They'd been walking a while more and Grian's feet were really beginning to throb when they came to another dead end and the soft Glimmer light fell across an old rusted door in the tunnel wall ahead. Beside the door a metal wire hung down from the ceiling. Attached to the bottom of it was a tiny pulley. Grian's dad yanked the wire.

"Now we wait," he told them, a slight smile playing round the edges of his lips.

A few minutes later, there was a clang and clatter, before a hatch in the centre of the door slid across. Grian could see the shadowed eyes and nose of a face beyond.

"Who is it?" the person whispered, their bristly bearded mouth now in the centre of the hatch.

"It's me. Cam Woods," Grian's dad replied, standing back far enough so the person could get a good look.

There were more clangs and clatters before a loud squeak of rusted hinges filled the space. The door opened, spilling light across a slice of the dark tunnel.

"Cam," the man said, wrapping him in a huge bear hug. "You had us worried, mate!"

"I've brought guests, Arthur." His dad turned round and beckoned the others forward.

Grian gulped, stepping into the light. He was the most wanted boy in Babbage. Should his dad really be introducing him to any of his work friends?

"Oh, my boy!" Arthur grabbed Grian's shoulders like a vice and bent down so he was eye to eye with him. "You and your friends are heroes!"

"Heroes?" Grian whispered, the word slipping like a question off his lips.

"Yes!" Arthur smiled, standing back up, his broad frame filling the doorway. "Now, how do you need our help?"

"What do ya mean our help?" Shelli asked, surprised.

"Come on, I'll show you." Arthur turned and started walking up a set of steps behind him.

Grian shrugged and was the first to follow his dad out through the door and up the winding stone staircase behind Arthur. At the top, they came to another old door. Arthur opened it and stepped through onto a black, white and red marble floor.

Grian was in awe. Far above his head was a vast domed ceiling, covered in decorative white plaster coving and held up by numerous large marble columns. Hanging between the columns were huge chandeliers, casting tiny rainbows round the walls as light caught in their delicate glass pieces. The building looked important, like something he'd probably learn about in history class. The only giveaway that this was a post office were the various bits of signage branded *BPO*, for Babbage Post Office.

Though the doors to the public looked to be locked,

the huge building was really busy. People rushed back and forth across the marble floor, carrying bits of paper and chatting in hushed tones to their colleagues.

A large TV screen hung above a circular, carved, wooden helpdesk in the middle of the open space. A group of postal workers stood under the screen looking up at it, their eyes fixed to the rolling news items that flashed by regularly.

Another group gathered around a huge map of Babbage attached to the wall at the other side of the room. The map was covered in lots and lots of red flags that they seemed to be discussing in detail.

Everyone wore the same navy uniform Grian's dad always wore for work, with the gold *BPO* lettering embroidered on the shirt pocket. And though some people in the place wore Hansoms, it struck Grian as odd that most appeared to have taken theirs off; the band of lighter skin on their wrists a giveaway.

"Friends, I need your attention," Arthur bellowed, his huge voice echoing round the enormous space. "I'd like you to meet some friends of ours."

Every face in the room turned towards them. Grian gulped and hid behind his father's back.

"Is that Cam and... It's them! Grian, Shelli, Jeffrey," a dark-haired lady raced up and threw her arms around all three of them, "you children are the bravest people

I know. Thank you so much for taking on this battle and for trying to save our planet. We are with you all the way, whatever we can do."

The woman had tears in her eyes as she hugged each one of them separately. Others had circled round them now too and were desperately trying to shake the children's hands or pat them on the back.

"'We'?" Grian questioned, looking up at Arthur.

"Yes, we." The man nodded back. "We're the Postal Network and we are at your service! Together we'll find these letters and stop Howard Hansom."

"And they say the post is dead!" Grian's dad clapped as a huge cheer erupted round the massive space.

For the first time in what seemed like for ever, Grian felt like the world wasn't against them and that they weren't battling alone. Maybe, with help like this, they really might save the world.

When the excitement died down and the postal workers got back to work, Arthur took their group across to the map of Babbage mounted on the wall and dotted in red flags.

"These are the areas we've searched for letters. There've been some false leads, but so far we've found nothing else since the letter we handed over to you, Cam." Arthur lowered his voice speaking to Grian's dad. "We're scouring everywhere. Most postmen and -women are onboard now, but some still think we're on a wild goose chase. I expect that will change now though—"

"Why would it change now?" Shelli butted in.

"Oh, I bet you haven't seen it yet. Well you're in for a treat!" Arthur turned and strode back across to the large screen in the centre of the room.

"Pull up the video on hChirp," he asked a woman sitting at the round helpdesk.

The woman swiped across her hTablet and the screen hanging above them changed to a page on the hChirp platform with the handle @Mushka.

"That's our Mushka!" Jeffrey gasped.

"*I am not anyone's Mushka,*" their friend growled in their EarPods.

The woman then scrolled down to the most recent chirp on Mushka's page, which was a video, and pressed the play button.

The footage Jeffrey had taken of Howard Hansom in the warehouse with Vermilion only an hour or so before began to play on the large screen. It played in a loop, in which Hansom repeated over and over again:

"*I might destroy the mirror when I get back. I want to have a closer look at it first – I feel a plan forming. But I still need the White Rose's remaining letters! This will go down as the biggest achievement in history. I am a real-life Noah, and I will do whatever necessary to secure my ark. While the rest of the planet and everyone on it slips mindlessly towards death, I am the only one clever and brave enough to cut the fodder and save the cream of the crop, the elites of humanity.*

"I am moulding a future where human life won't just go on for millennia but, without bloodlines corrupted by the ignorant masses, it will thrive! It is vital we make sure there are no loose ends, or the earthquake and the Tipping Point and PEOPLEPOWER and all our work will have been for nothing; we will never steal the sun and everything we've been planning for years, not to mention our very existence as a species, will be destroyed."

"Oh my!" Jeffrey gasped, cupping his mouth.

"And it's already had over one million views. The Hansom company took it down, but it's been reposted so many times to so many different social networks they'd have to take down the whole hNet at this stage to stop it," Arthur told them cheerily. "People are beginning to question now, they're waking up. It won't be long before the tides turn in our favour. Whoever Mushka is, they're a genius."

"They truly are!" Jeffrey gushed.

"Hansom's just gone viral," Mushka laughed down the line. *"Now let's show him the ignorant masses mean business!"*

CHAPTER 33

THE LIGHT ORBS

Grian munched on a sandwich from a plate of food one of the post office workers had given them, while staring up at the map of Babbage, in awe at all the work the Postal Network had already put in to find the letters.

Once full, Jeffrey and Grian told Grian's dad and Arthur about what they'd heard in the warehouse and how it seemed Hansom himself had one of the White Rose's letters.

"Then there's only one letter left unaccounted for," Arthur said. "We've found the black mirror letter. Somehow we'll have to find out what Hansom's letter says, and there's one out there somewhere still to be found. Adler told you there were three letters – isn't that right, Cam?"

"Yeah." Grian's dad nodded. "Only one needle left in the haystack. Well, if anyone can find it the Postal Network can!"

Only Grian, Shelli, Jeffrey, Yarrow and now Mushka knew there were in fact four letters.

As his dad and Arthur spoke in hushed tones about further plans, Grian toyed seriously with telling them about Grandad's secret letter and the crystal. But something told him he shouldn't. Hansom suspected there was a fourth letter now too, because of what Vermilion had overheard in Dunstan. What if he found out the fourth letter really did exist? The more Hansom knew, the bigger the risk there was for the White Rose and their plans.

"We need to get going," Shelli whispered, swallowing a bite of her apple. "Amergin and Mother are almost at the hForest."

Nach was uneasy and started to whimper beside her.

"*Yes, Zaffre says they are almost there too,*" Mushka added.

"Dad, we have to go," Grian said, pulling on his father's sleeve.

"Where do you need to go?" Arthur asked eagerly. "We'll help you whatever way we can."

"To the hForest just outside of Hopper City," Grian replied.

"Right you are," the man said, pulling out a set of keys from his pocket. "We'll take my post van. You won't be spotted in the back."

It took them longer than it should have to leave the post office, as people patted the children on the back or stopped to shake their hands and give them words of encouragement. Grian felt famous, just like he did the night in the Tipping Point when Hansom threw them a celebratory party for saving his life. But this time, unlike the night in the Tipping Point, he was comfortable with the praise; it gave him hope.

The gestures were a show of support, a way for the Postal Network to let them know that they were all in this fight together.

When the last person had wished them good luck, Arthur led them out through a back door of the old postal building to a car park.

It was early evening and growing quickly dark.

Rows and rows of navy blue vans with gold *BPO* lettering were parked up. Arthur pressed a button on his keys and one of the vans beeped as it reversed out of its space a few metres away and drove itself round to them.

"There she is," Arthur said, opening up the double doors at the back. "Everyone in, quickly."

Grian hunched down a little, bent his head and shuffled inside. It was a tight squeeze with Shelli, Jeffrey, his dad and Nach all squashed in the back together.

"I'll get you as close as I can to the edge of the hForest," Arthur said, before closing the doors and locking them all in.

"If Arthur wanted to, he could surrender us all up right now and there is nothing any of us could do about it," Jeffrey stated. "With perhaps the exception of you, Shelli – I imagine you could conjure your animals or somesuch."

"*Hey! I could do something too – remotely,*" Mushka said, sounding a little offended.

Grian shivered as the engine started. He watched through glimpses of the front window while they drove smoothly out onto a quiet road. After a few minutes they passed the museum, where there was still a bit of activity and police tape cordoned off the entrance.

The streets of Hopper City looked a little more chaotic than they had that morning. It was hard to explain, but the atmosphere seemed to have shifted – people appeared less sure of where they were heading or what they were doing.

"It's almost as if they've lost their schedules," Grian whispered.

"Have you noticed too?" Jeffrey replied. "It's odd, isn't it? It's almost as if their Hansoms aren't working. Which can't be possible, surely? No matter what I personally think of Howard Hansom, his technology is second to none – unless the signals have gone down again?"

"Or maybe people just aren't listening to their watches as much any more?" Shelli answered.

"*They're not,*" Mushka said into their ears. "*There are viral videos of people taking their watches off and breaking them. Hansom is losing trust since his little speech almost broke the hNet. It's like a revolution's happening.*"

"I can feel there's an energy building," Shelli almost whispered, her amber eyes alive. "It only takes a small wind to make a wave."

Grian took a deep breath, and his body tingled. Something good and big was happening: people were waking up to Hansom's lies, he could feel it.

The van continued out of the centre of town, past the housing estates and then wound its way up the hill until Arthur pulled over into a lay-by. Grian could see the gravel path they'd walked down only the night before.

"Right. Good luck then!" Arthur said, turning round in his seat to look at them. "We are here if you want us. Our communications team at the Postal Network has made contact with Mushka and she'll let us know if you're in need of our help."

Then the large man climbed from the front and his feet crunched on the gravel as he walked round to open the back doors. Everyone crawled awkwardly out. Grian was the last to leave the safety of the van. He shivered a little at the thought of all they'd been through and all that possibly lay ahead.

"You kids are an inspiration." Arthur's voice broke, locking watery eyes with each one of them.

Grian felt awkward. He had never seen such a big man cry.

"Take care of yourselves." Arthur managed to squeeze out the words as he wrapped all three of them in another huge bear hug. "And you too, Cam," he said, standing upright again and slapping Grian's dad on the shoulder.

"Thanks, Arthur – take care of yourself too, and the team," Grian's dad replied solemnly.

Then without another word, Arthur wiped his eyes, climbed into the van and drove off back towards Hopper City.

In the silence left behind, Grian could hear the buzz of the hForest. The incessant sound penetrated right into his skull. He'd grown to hate the fake trees.

Shelli and Nach were the first to head up the gravel path into the hForest, followed by Jeffrey, Grian and his dad. Though it was almost dark, Shelli didn't light her Glimmer.

Grian's heart pounded and he felt sick, as the low buzz itched at his skin.

Every time he passed a real tree, he touched its bark

and a deep sense of comfort and calm washed through him. Though he was sure he imagined it, it felt like the real tree trunks almost bowed towards him at his touch.

Normally the digital forests were dead to most life but strangely right now, the place was alive with the sounds of creatures, and Grian almost stepped on a badger that scuttled passed his feet.

"Don't squish our army," Shelli joked.

"What do you mean 'army'?" he asked.

"Can't you see? They know what we're doing and they want to help. Animals hate de hForests, they make them sick. But they've come here now to help us. They're fighting back too."

Grian felt like his whole heart swelled and swallowed his body. He looked around, his lip trembling. Shelli was right: the branches of the trees were full of birds and animals, while their thick trunks teemed with insects. The usually dead undergrowth of the hForest crawled with all sorts of creatures: some furry, some scaly and more still slimy.

"I suppose it makes rather good sense," Jeffrey replied, a family of butterflies fluttering round his face. "After all, they have more than a passing interest. It is their planet too."

"Shush..." Grian's dad held up his hand. "I hear something."

Shelli crouched, signalling for everyone to duck down too. A dark figure leaned against a tree trunk in a clearing ahead.

Shelli had just crawled forward a little closer when Grian's dad stopped her.

"No. You three stay here. I'll go see who it is. If anything happens, run!" he whispered.

Shelli growled. She clearly didn't want to be held back.

Grian could barely watch his dad walk forward through the thick trees. When he reached the clearing, the figure stepped out into the dusk light.

"Cam!" Yarrow said, rushing to embrace him. "We've been so worried!"

Grian climbed from his hiding spot and raced forward too. When he reached the clearing, other figures were emerging slowly from the shadows. Zaffre walked to Yarrow's side and Amergin held Mother's hand as they stepped into the faint light just behind Zaffre.

"Zaffre, Yarrow!" Grian stuttered, almost tripping over himself in his hurry to get to them. "Vermilion betrayed us. He's – he's with Hansom! He tried to steal the black mirror from us…"

"We know. Mushka told Zaffre. I…I still can't believe it," Yarrow muttered, before her voice fell almost to a whisper. "And the mirror, is it okay?"

"Yes, I think so," Shelli answered, handing over her rucksack to Yarrow.

As Yarrow pulled out the mirror and discussed what had happened with the others, Amergin stepped closer to Shelli and seemed to study her face.

"You've been worried about your visions, child. I can tell," he said softly.

Shelli nodded, tears in her eyes.

"I've seen the sun go fully black – like de end of de world," she whispered, trembling. "Since you touched my forehead in your forest, I see things like that and I don't want to."

"I passed you some of my gift, Shelli. But you need to learn how to use it. Your visions are not real, always remember that. They are only possibilities. Call them stories, even. They may or may not become real, depending on our decisions. You will learn to put your energy into de visions you wish to make reality – that's de mark of a great Seer."

Then Amergin stepped forward and hugged her so hard her face disappeared into his black feather waistcoat.

"Thank you," Shelli mumbled, when he stepped back and smiled.

"Can I have de black mirror?" Amergin asked, turning to Yarrow. "Mother filled me in when we met. Let's see what secrets are held inside this obsidian glass. I fear time is not on our side tonight."

Amergin took the mirror in one hand. With his other hand, he held Shelli's wrist.

Except for the buzz of the trees, the whole forest – including the army of creatures who'd gathered in the clearing – fell into total silence.

The Wilde Seer stared deep into the black mirror and appeared to enter into a trance-like state. His grip on Shelli tightened, and she closed her eyes.

Grian watched, almost afraid to breathe. Amergin's grip tightened further on Shelli's wrist until both their arms vibrated in unison and their features contorted in deep concentration. Then, from nowhere, a smile warmed both their faces.

The creatures in the clearing came back alive, making more noise than ever. Grian gasped in awe. The birds who watched from the surrounding trees began to flap their wings and sing. The squirrels jumped noisily from branch to branch. The mice and rabbits and badgers and moles and many creatures he had no name for caused a ruckus on the forest floor, while a sea of insects created beautiful wave-like formations across the tree trunks, reflecting the light of the setting sun.

Then, just as suddenly as it started up, everything stopped and total stillness settled on the clearing.

Grian's chest expanded and his shoulders dropped.

A feeling he had never experienced washed over him. His mind emptied, his constantly racing heart relaxed and he was filled with a deep sense of love, total joy and wonder. He looked around him. Every person and creature seemed to be overtaken by the same feeling, as wide smiles swept across the faces of his friends.

Then he blinked twice, in case his eyes weren't working properly. A bright orb about the size of his fist hovered out from his chest into the air. It stopped directly in front of him and spun and danced gently from side to side. He moved his hands up to touch it but his fingers slipped right through.

It reminded Grian of the circle of light that appeared in the middle of the Glimmer every time Shelli lit it, and he was totally mesmerized by the beauty of this simple luminous ball.

Staring through the translucent centre of his own orb, he noticed everyone else had their own orb too, floating exactly like his, chest high in front of their body. And it wasn't only the humans who had them, it was every creature, from the tiniest ant to the largest bird. Even the real trees, flowers and grasses had orbs of their own, so the forest was filled with thousands of light balls dancing gently like fireflies in the dusk.

Amergin's light was different to the others though. His orb started to grow so big it engulfed his whole body, until he was standing inside it, still holding Shelli's wrist. The old man's eyes were closed and his smile was large.

Shelli, who was standing just outside Amergin's light, wasn't smiling any more though. While her eyes were still closed, tears streamed down her cheeks.

Grian moved to comfort his friend, but Mother grabbed his hand.

"Don't," she whispered, shaking her head.

Suddenly the animals grew frantic and wild. Some pawed at the ground, clearly distressed, as others made loud, terrifying noises. The calm that had fallen over them all fled. Grian covered his ears, his mind racing. His orb darted back inside his body. He looked around – everyone else's orbs had vanished inside them too.

"You need to get out of here. Something is wrong," Yarrow told him. "Take this." She grabbed Shelli's rucksack from the ground and dropped an object inside it, before shoving the bag into Grian's arms. "It's up to you three now. Go!"

Just then dark, caped figures floated silently out of the trees to circle the group in the clearing like a ring of black ghosts.

"Excuse the hood, but it seems it's a necessity out here in the wider world, since your little hChirp trick," Howard Hansom snarled, throwing back the oversized hood of his black cloak. He hovered a metre or so from the forest floor directly opposite Grian. "I must give it to you all. You were quite clever, solving that letter the postmen found. When Vermilion told me what it said, I must admit I was stumped for a while. I did work out the black mirror, but 'the Poet' – that got me. Wilde beliefs and superstitions aren't my thing. Thankfully you figured it out for me."

Everyone moved further into the centre of the clearing, the Proctors tightening their circle round the group. Grian looked around for a way to escape, his heart pounding once more.

"Now give me the mirror and the Poet, and be quick," Hansom continued. "There are much more important things happening tonight that need my attention."

"No," Amergin said. The wide smile had vanished from his bearded face. "Stop this destruction now. You don't understand de natural forces you are playing with."

"I understand all too well what I am doing, old man. Maybe it is you who doesn't understand. But perhaps a look in that mirror will clear things up for you. It will for me, anyway – with luck it'll even lead me to this mysterious White Rose. Now take him!" Hansom ordered his Proctors.

The Proctors moved towards Amergin, who immediately flung the black mirror into the air. Just then a huge black hawk swept down low into the clearing, like a winged shadow, and caught the mirror in its large beak.

"Stop that creature!" Hansom cried.

A cloaked Proctor beside Hansom threw their arm forward with such force that their hood fell off, revealing Vermilion beneath.

"I trusted you!" Yarrow yelled fiercely at the man, as a huge wave of energy surged from Vermilion's gloved fist after the bird.

"No!" Amergin howled, flinging himself directly into the path of the powerful wave.

The Wilde Seer screamed, hit in the chest by the invisible force. His body tumbled backward through the air before walloping against a digital tree. A deep gasp of pain left his lips before he collapsed in silence.

"Amergin!" Shelli roared, racing to the Poet's side.

Chaos took over the hForest.

The Proctors struggled to keep afloat, attacked from all sides by every animal and insect in sight. As the creatures clawed, scratched, bit and stung Hansom and his men, Mother reached her arms skywards, cast her head back and released a deep guttural cry. The sound was unearthly, unlike anything Grian had ever heard before.

Suddenly a loud clap of thunder rang through the area and forks of lightning stabbed the ground. Sparks of electricity flew through the air from some of the fake trees; others burst into flames. The wind picked up and the real trees dotted through the hForest seemed to swing their thick branches for the Proctors.

"Children, you need to run!" Mother yelled over the gusting wind that swept her white hair. "You need to run now! We will hold them off. Go. You *will* save the world, you just need to believe it."

Grian grabbed Shelli's arm and tried to drag her from Amergin, whose breathing was now sparse and shallow. She struggled against him until Jeffrey grabbed her other arm and together they pulled her away.

"We have to go, we have to go," Grian cried, his heart pounding.

He was sprinting out of the clearing, his friends by his side, when suddenly he stumbled, and an invisible force buckled his legs beneath him. Grian fell and was dragged backwards across the forest floor. He scrambled his arms against the dirt, desperately trying to claw himself onward, when his whole body was flipped violently over so he was staring up at the night sky.

He cried out in terror as a dark figure flew through the air towards him like a hunter about to pounce on prey. Howard Hansom stopped right above him, only his face visible beneath the billowing black cloak.

He glared down at Grian.

"You didn't think I'd let you get away? Since my plan

to have the whole world distracted looking for you and your friends seems to have fallen apart, I've come up with another use for you now." The man's eyes were wild and he seemed almost crazed. "I thought I'd break your grandfather and he'd tell me what he knows about the White Rose, but it still seems the old man won't talk. I bet he'd talk if he saw how good I was at torturing his favourite grandson though. And if he still won't talk – I know you will, Grian. You'll be in so much pain, you'll tell me everything about this secret fourth letter."

Grian's heart raced and sweat dripped down his brow as he tried to struggle away, but he couldn't shift against the unseen force. His legs felt trapped inside an invisible cord.

"I'll start the torture with something like this," the man laughed.

Hansom's hand appeared from under the cape, the black rubber of the hThoughtTech glove he wore clearly visible. Slowly he curled his fingers inwards and closed his open fist, as if squeezing the air.

Grian screamed out. The pain that ripped through his legs from the sudden intense pressure was almost unbearable. It felt like they were in a vice, and every bone was just about to shatter. He roared and wriggled in agony, tears streaming down his face.

This was it: this was how his life ended.

Through the haze of agony, a deep growling reached his ears. Then Hansom turned and shouted in surprise as a number of foxes pounced on him.

The man stumbled forward onto Grian.

The pressure lifted. Grian's legs were freed. He scrambled backwards from underneath Hansom, while Nach, who led the frenzy of foxes, ripped and tore at the large hood of the man's cloak.

"Get up, Grian!" Jeffrey shouted.

His friends were beside him, pulling frantically at his arms to yank him onto his feet. Then they were running again. Grian's thoughts jumbled in the chaos. They had just broken free of the clearing when a blood-curdling cry cut the air.

Shelli stopped.

"Nach!" she screamed, turning to race back.

"You can't go back... We have to go on, Shelli. It's not Nach, there were quite a few foxes back there. She'll be fine – think of the sun," Jeffrey stuttered, pulling desperately on her arm.

Grian joined Jeffrey and together they tried to convince Shelli.

She struggled against them, but when their words finally seeped through, she moved forward with her friends in a daze.

Screams, cries, crashes and bangs filled the hForest,

from the battle still raging behind them. Grian didn't dare look back or think about his dad or Nach or Amergin or the others as his lungs heaved and they pushed away through the trees.

"Quickly! In here," Jeffrey said after they'd been running a while, his voice barely reaching through the fog of Grian's mind.

His friend was standing waist-high in a big hollow that was hidden by thick roots at the base of a large real tree. The hollow was concealed by overhanging vines, making it a perfect hiding place. Jeffrey squeezed in first, then helped Grian to coax Shelli down.

They sat there for hours, between periods of fitful sleep, until the morning began to ink into the sky.

CHAPTER 34

ADABELLE

"Grian, Jeffrey, Shelli, can anyone hear me?" Mushka's voice sounded muffled in their EarPods.

Jeffrey was the first to reply. "Oh, Mushka! Yes, affirmative – thank heavens. I didn't know where you'd gone to. Is everything in working order? You sound distant."

"No, the signals are coming and going all over Hopper. I couldn't reach you guys for hours. It's back up and running now, but it's patchy. I can't reach Zaffre at all, his watch seems to be offline. Have you seen him or the others?"

"No, we had to r-run. Some of the hForest was d-destroyed. There were fires," Grian stuttered, trying to block out the images that played over in his mind. "Maybe that's why the signals are out?"

"*What happened? Are you guys okay?*" Mushka asked, her voice a little high-pitched.

"Hansom and Vermilion showed up with the Proctors..." Jeffrey answered. "Things got a little out of hand."

"Out of hand! That doesn't describe it at all, Jeffrey," Grian replied, stumbling through his terrifying memories. "It was awful – so scary! We lost the mirror, and there was fighting. Yarrow and Zaffre and Mother were there – she told us to run – and Dad, I don't know where Dad is... And Amergin was hit by Vermilion, he didn't look good. Hansom attacked me – we barely got away. Nach and the foxes saved me. I hope...I hope they're okay."

There was a short intake of breath on the other end of their EarPods. The three friends stared at each other; each looked a little more broken than they had the day before. Unsure what to do or how to help his friends or himself, Grian reached his arms round both their shoulders and hugged them. It wasn't hard in the cramped space.

"*Surely you guys aren't saying that it's over, though...*" Mushka said after a moment. "*Like it's the end of the road and we're all doomed kinda stuff? Like the BBEG has won. Is that where you're going with this?*"

"No," Shelli said, speaking for the first time. She looked suddenly fierce, masking her pain. "We're still going to save de world. Hansom will not win. And he will pay for whatever he's done to Nach. I don't care what happens to me, but I care what happens to yous and all de Wilde and everyone and everything on this planet. This is not de end."

"I care dearly what happens to you all too," Jeffrey answered solemnly, "but I'm afraid I also care for what happens to me. I mean, if I don't care for my own well-being, how will I ever be able to care for anyone else?"

"*Profound as usual, Jef!*" Mushka joked, breaking the tension.

"We need to go back and find Amergin – we need to know what the mirror showed him," Grian said, thinking out loud.

"He's gone," Shelli whispered, her lower lip trembling now. "I think he planned it that way – so Hansom couldn't use him to look in the mirror if they were captured. He's dead. I'm sure of it… I saw it in a vision when he held my wrist."

"What… But the mirror – we need to know what it revealed…" Jeffrey stuttered, a little shell-shocked.

Grian stayed silent. Amergin was dead? He'd never known a dead person. He couldn't process what that meant, or how it made him feel inside. There was a strange emptiness – a hollow where feeling had been.

"*In my heart the battle is won,*" Shelli said, so lightly it was hard to hear.

"What?" Grian asked, snapping back a little.

"It's the last line of the White Rose's riddle. Amergin passed me all his gift of Seeing," she said. "He grabbed my wrist in de clearing and showed me what's hidden in de mirror. How to save de sun.

"We need to find her. Right now she's in a bed. She's old, with long white hair. She looks like she's sleeping but she's not sleeping. I think. It's hard to tell, de visions came in flashes."

"Who's 'she'?" Grian asked.

"De White Rose," Shelli said, like the answer were obvious.

Grian and Jeffrey gasped.

"You actually saw her?" Grian said.

Shelli closed her eyes, before speaking again.

"We need to bring de White Rose to a weird curved glass place with thousands of chairs. I saw three shadows standing round her as she lay in one of those chairs. A letter leads to these three people. She loves them, and they need to be there in de end.

"She also needs to be holding two objects in her hands, and there is a letter for each of those objects."

"So we have to find two objects and three people, and take them to the White Rose?" Grian wondered aloud, "Maybe the black mirror is one of those objects?"

"No," Shelli shook her head, "the black mirror is our guide. And we have to get it back."

"One of those objects must be the crystal that accompanied Grian's grandfather's secret letter?" Jeffrey speculated.

"*I think now's the time you guys fill me in on this secret letter!*" Mushka announced.

Grian told Mushka about grandad's letter as the other two listened.

"*So let me get this straight. There's four letters, not three. One was given in secret to your grandad with a crystal, one led us to the black mirror, Hansom has one which led him to your grandad, and there's still one to find,*" Mushka said after Grian finished.

"Exactly!" Jeffrey answered. "So the letter still to find must lead to the second object the White Rose needs in her hand, Shelli?"

"Yeah maybe, Jeffrey," Shelli said, still half dazed. "My head hurts – all I can think about is Nach."

"*Where do we find the White Rose?*" Mushka pushed.

"I don't know," Shelli answered, a little frustrated. "I do remember though that outside de window where she is right now I could see de sun – it was full and bright and there wasn't a single black mark on it."

"Then the mirror was lying." Jeffrey shook his head. "Your vision cannot be real!"

"It was real," Shelli growled. "The mirror wasn't lying…"

"A strange sky…" Grian said, remembering back.

300

"Grandad said something about a strange sky too, when I heard his voice on the hSwarm app, just after Hansom took him."

"*Did you see anything else in the mirror that might help us find her?*" Mushka pressed again.

"Yes, there was a picture on de wall in de room where she's waiting for us now... It's all hazy and in flashes. It's hard to tell but...I don't know, but..."

"But what?" Grian encouraged Shelli when she hesitated.

"Well, I don't know for sure. I mean, it all happened so fast, but I think I recognize the picture..."

"*Woah! You serious?*" Mushka said, surprised.

"Well, yeah... I'd need to look in de black mirror again to be certain, but I think I've seen de picture before. Three young girls are sitting in de middle of a forest. All of them have white hair and white eyebrows... I don't know, maybe I'm wrong... Like I said, all I can really think about right now is Nach..."

Grian was about to say something consoling when Shelli brushed him off and climbed out of the hollow. He watched, confused, as she shot up the tree they'd been sitting under until her slight figure was just a dark shadow against the moonlight.

"I expect she needs some space – she's clearly worried," Jeffrey whispered.

Grian stood and climbed out of their cramped hiding spot too. His legs were stiff and sore but they had to get moving. He also needed, though he wasn't sure he wanted, to see what had happened back in the clearing. He needed to know what had happened to his dad.

He was just stretching his legs when there was a soft thud. Shelli landed on the ground beside him.

"I can see smoke in that direction." Her lip quivered again. She was pointing back the way they had come. "But there is no other movement. I can sense Mother, I think she's okay, but I can't sense Nach. I know we really need to get going, I want to save the sun, but...but first..."

"But first we have to go back," Grian finished her sentence.

Without another word, he turned and walked through the fake trees in the direction of the smoke.

He knew Shelli was worried and he wasn't leaving either without looking for his dad. What if he was hurt somewhere in the forest? What if he needed their help?

"But what if the Proctors or Hansom are still there... lying in wait?" Jeffrey stuttered.

Grian didn't respond – he couldn't think about what was possibly waiting for them back in the clearing.

Jeffrey hesitated for a minute before joining his friends.

As they travelled back the way they had come, the

buzzing of the hForest was intermittent, like the digital trees were in need of repair.

"All this time in the hForest has given me a new appreciation for real trees and your Wilde home, Shelli," Jeffrey said, after a spark of electricity darted across the early morning sky from a cracked trunk beside him.

"That's it!" Shelli gasped, stopping dead. "I think I know why that picture I saw in de White Rose's room is familiar. It's hanging in de meeting hut in my forest too! Well, an embroidery of it is. Do you remember de wall hanging in de hut? On one part of it there are three young white-haired girls sitting in a forest."

"But why would the White Rose also have that picture?" Jeffrey wondered.

"Well, we said we thought she could be Wilde..." Shelli answered, thinking out loud.

Suddenly Grian remembered the picture he'd taken yesterday in the museum, and opened the photo app on his watch.

"I took this yesterday after we'd stolen the mirror," he said, quickly swiping. "I knew it reminded me of something."

He showed the image to his friends. The picture of the circus characters was black and white but browned by time. Sitting cross-legged at the front of the colourful crowd were three young white-haired girls.

He zoomed in on the information card typed under the picture.

This is one of the last photos of the Belle Sisters from the famous travelling circus the Barnaby Brothers. The sisters disappeared shortly after this was taken.

"De Belle Sisters!" Shelli said, staring down at his watch. "That's de circus act Mother was in! And de girls in this picture, Grian, are de same girls as de ones in de picture in de White Rose's room, and in de meeting hut. I'm sure of it. Mother is one of those girls – Mam told me that once. The other two are her sisters."

"Adabelle, Adorabelle and Aristabelle were three young girls with albinism called the Belle Sisters, who were a famous circus act that disappeared from the Barnaby Brothers' circus." Mushka sounded as if she was reading from something. *"There's stuff about them on the hNet."*

"Adorabelle," Jeffrey interrupted. "That's Howard Hansom's mother's name. Surely that's not a hugely popular name? I mean, I have certainly never met an Adorabelle before. Could it merely be a coincidence, or could Howard Hansom's mother actually be the White Rose after all? Now that would be quite the surprise!"

"Did Mother ever say anything to you about Howard Hansom's mam being her sister?" Grian quizzed Shelli.

"No. She doesn't really talk about her sisters at all," the girl replied.

"I found an article online, written years ago, about Howard Hansom's mother," Mushka cut in. "It says she is originally from the Wilde forest in Tallystick and that she had two sisters. She is albino too – this is epic but it's adding up. I'm sending you a picture now of Adorabelle Hansom. See what you think, Shelli. You saw her in the black mirror – is she the White Rose?"

A little shaky and unsure how to really use the device Mushka had given her, Shelli stared down at Grian's watch. A picture of a striking, elegantly dressed older lady with sunglasses and sleeked-back short white hair appeared on screen. Adorabelle was dressed in an iridescent blue ballgown, and stood on a red carpet arm in arm with her tuxedo-clad son, Howard Hansom.

"No, she's not de White Rose," Shelli replied with certainty. "But she could definitely be her sister."

"Well if it's not Adorabelle and it's not Mother, then the White Rose must be the other girl in the picture!" Grian said, twitching with excitement.

"Yeah, I think so," Shelli replied, almost breathless. "Hansom's mam is Adorabelle, Mother's real name is Aristabelle – so de White Rose must be Adabelle. But Mother said she disappeared years ago…"

"Didn't Mother also say Adabelle, her youngest sister, made your Glimmer?" Grian asked, remembering their talk with Mother in the Wilde hut just before they'd left a couple of days ago. "Your Glimmer acts exactly like the crystal Grandad was sent by the White Rose…"

"*Woah, that is seriously extra!*" Mushka announced, thumping something loudly.

"It can't merely be a coincidence," Jeffrey stated, "that the White Rose is Howard Hansom's aunt!"

"And now we really need to find her," Shelli replied, her amber eyes wild.

CHAPTER 35

RIDERS OF THE APOCALYPSE

"*There's no record of an Adabelle anywhere else on the hNet, except in relation to her and her sisters going missing, guys,*" Mushka said, as the threesome walked onwards through the hForest.

"If we figure out how Adabelle is connected to Grandad it might help us. Hansom said his letter led him to Grandad and two other people. They must be the three people the White Rose loves, the people you saw in the mirror, Shelli – so Adabelle loves Grandad but..." Grian was thinking aloud, when suddenly a large black shadow crossed the sky and swooped down into a clearing ahead.

"Amergin's hawk – he has de mirror!" Shelli said, racing forward.

Grian chased after her, breaking into the clearing just in time to see the huge bird drop the black shiny disc straight into Shelli's hands.

Grian's relief at the mirror's return was immediately swallowed up by the devastation around him. They were back in the same place they had fled in horror the night before.

Some of the digital trees were split in half or lying at awkward angles, and sparks flew readily from them into the air. The outer plastic shell of other trees had melted like candle wax, revealing their steel and wire innards.

Grian covered his mouth with his T-shirt to avoid choking on the burned plastic-soaked air.

"There's no one here." He trembled, sitting down next to a smouldering trunk. "Dad and the others – they've gone!"

"But where have they gone?" Jeffrey looked around, bewildered. "Do you think Hansom has captured them?"

Shelli searched the clearing, ignoring the others.

"What if he's hurt them?" Grian said, his mind spinning out of control.

"I can't find Nach..." Shelli's angst cut through his panic.

Her face was pale and her hands were shaking. It was one of the only times Grian could remember seeing his friend so vulnerable. Nach was Shelli's world.

Without another word, the two boys joined her search.

Forgetting their fear of Hansom's return, all three children cried out desperately for Nach. They trundled through the devastation for what seemed like ages, lifting up fallen branches and stepping round sizzling wires.

As every second ticked by, the knot in Grian's stomach twisted tighter.

Then a distant whimper grew slowly louder. There was rustling in the undergrowth until a small fragile fox moved out of the shadows into the clearing.

"Nach!" Shelli cried.

She raced forward, catching the fox in her arms as the creature collapsed.

Nach's breathing was heavy. Her whimpers frequent and painful.

"Oh my!" Jeffrey exclaimed. "I suspect this might be the cause of her discomfort."

He moved his hand through Nach's thick bloody fur to reveal a gash along the side of her back leg. The fox began to shiver. Shelli grew visibly upset, and seemed unable to think.

"What can we do? She needs help!" Grian whispered, panicked, to Jeffrey. "We're in the middle of nowhere…"

Suddenly the area began to fill up, just like the evening before. Creatures great and small entered the clearing and formed a tight circle round the three friends.

"Please, she needs your help!" Grian's eyes welled in tears.

It felt weird, but right, speaking openly to the animals.

A large fox stepped through the circle and began to lick Nach's injured back leg, as a squirrel – who been chewing some kind of plant – stepped forward too. Once the fox had finished, the squirrel spat out the plant onto its tiny palm and began to gently rub the substance along the wound. Then Grian noticed slug-like insects appearing out of the ground. The creatures climbed up Nach's red fur and the fox whimpered when they wriggled onto the open wound.

"I think they're leeches," Jeffrey said, amazed. "If I'm not mistaken, we humans used them as medicine in more primitive times, for pain relief and to treat infection."

Some of the animals prepared a bed of soft moss and leaves in the shadows, and as Nach's whimpering eased, Shelli moved her out of the clearing onto it. All three watched her fall into a peaceful sleep, before returning to the clearing.

"She just needs to rest for a bit." Shelli sighed, relieved, "She'll be okay now."

"Shelli," Grian whispered. "The balls of light that came out of our chests last night and made me feel so peaceful and calm. They came out of all the animals too. What were they?"

"De light orbs are our energy. Every living thing has one. Some people call it a soul. Amergin called it love," Shelli said. "Amergin was showing me how de light orbs have something to do with how Hansom is stealing de sun, but then de Proctors turned up and he stopped."

Shelli bent down and picked the black mirror off the ground, where she'd dropped it when Nach appeared. Then she took her rucksack from Grian and opened it to place the mirror inside.

"How did this get in here?" she asked, pulling out a small cream drawstring bag.

Grian gasped. He took the small bag from her hand and opened it. The citrine crystal and letter were still tucked neatly inside, the same as they had been the day his grandfather handed the bag to him in the Tipping Point.

"I forgot Yarrow threw something into the rucksack when Hansom and his Proctors surrounded us in the forest... This must have been it. She gave the rucksack to me and said it was up to us three now..." Grian said hesitantly, remembering.

"I suspect she meant it was up to us three to save the world," Jeffrey interrupted.

"*Guys, guys, you have got to read this!*" Mushka's voice sounded excited in their EarPods. "*I've been looking at a very interesting thread on hReadit the last while. I didn't want* to say anything until I was sure, but I think we might have hit the big time..."

A screenshot appeared on Grian's watch, and his heart skipped a beat.

Posted by PatSOn 4 hours ago
Hey guys. Good one for u. Think I have one of Howard Hansom's famous letters – the ones everyone seems to be talking about since that video on hChirp. No JOKE!!!! My dad's a postman and he's bin lookin for these letters for ages. He'll kill me if he knows I've done this, but come on – the White Rose – I'm not buying it! It has to be a hoax. Anyway, see what you think – anyone good at puzzles!?

Underneath the text was a picture of an opened red envelope beside an unfolded letter. The envelope looked the same as the envelope the first letter the Postal Network found had been in. The writing on the letter looked the same too.

"*What you think?*" Mushka asked, breaking the stunned silence.

Grian didn't reply, he was too busy reading.

Dear Postman,
I'm a half-life in Atlantis waiting for the flood,

Or the righteous to be set free at the stilling of my
blood.

*You are all in Plato's cave, staring at the shadows
of the sun.*

*By the time you've seen your inner light, the world
we know will be done.*

*Unless you seek my stone half-heart; given when I
was young and scared*

*To a lettered man I loved, though for love I was ill
prepared.*

*When the last ray of sun has left and a terrifying
dawn about to flower,*

*Reignite my stone heart with its hessian twin, for
the magic hour.*

The White Rose

"I'd say it's real," Grian gulped. "But it's pretty
complicated! What does *'I'm a half-life in Atlantis'* even
mean? It'll take for ever to figure it out. It's time we don't
have!"

"*We don't need to figure it out,*" Mushka replied, sending
through a link to the thread. "*It's lighting up the hNet
already.*"

"But then Hansom will see this. He'll know it's real
too," Shelli gasped.

"*Nothing we can do about that now. It's already gone viral.*

There's no stopping it. We'll just have to beat Hansom to the prize," Mushka said.

Grian clicked on the link and scanned through the thread. There were already so many replies he could hardly keep up.

Posted by MrPuzzle333 24 minutes ago
In Plato's Cave, the philosopher Plato describes a group of people chained in a cave, facing a blank wall. The people watch shadows projected on the wall, and foolishly believe these shadows are the real objects... Clearly the White Rose is trying to tell us we are the fools. As if the WR knows the truth and we don't! Who is this person anyway?

Posted by Yourownway 24 minutes ago
And by the time we realize we're being fooled, the world is ended? Maybe this White Rose is talking about the sun. I mean, it's a bit freaky you guys. It's like almost half dark now. Nobody else scared about that, no matter what the Hansom corp says?

Posted by BobbieJo53 23 minutes ago
So the White Rose is underneath domed Atlantis skies, and Atlantis is a lost city...

Grian startled and looked up from his watch. A roar of

what sounded like hundreds of engines filled the air. Then there were voices in the forest not far away. Most of the animals in the area scattered.

"Hide," Shelli whispered, quickly racing through the clearing to Nach's side in the shadows.

Grian scrambled behind the thick trunk of a real tree. Jeffrey followed him and they both waited, watching. The voices grew louder until a large, bearded man wearing huge black boots, black leather trousers and a black leather jacket full of silver studs appeared in the clearing.

"What the..." he choked, stepping over a fallen digital tree. "Looks like there's been one hell of a fight here, folks!"

Grian held his breath, his heart thumping wildly. More leather-clad men and women walked around the clearing, kicking at the fake trees as they examined the scene. They all had the letters *ROTA* emblazoned in silver studs across the back of their jackets.

"Riders of the Apocalypse are a notorious biker gang," Jeffrey whispered.

"Notorious, are we?" a woman replied, standing above the pair.

Grian whipped round to look at her. She grabbed his top and pulled him roughly to standing.

The woman wore calf-high studded boots and her blonde hair was tied back in a red and white bandana. A similarly dressed man grabbed Jeffrey by the collar of his jumper and yanked him upright too.

Grian watched, terrified, as Shelli scampered silently up a tree nearby.

The gang crowded around Grian and Jeffrey, their surly expressions, huge tattoos, and leather-studded clothes intimidating.

"Did you boys make this mess?" the large man who'd been the first to walk into the clearing growled, slowly stroking his grizzly grey beard.

"No, we, ahem…we were merely bystanders to the occurrence," Jeffrey stuttered.

"Are you mocking me, boy!?" the man snarled into Jeffrey's face.

"Hey, it's them – the kids who wrecked the Tipping Point," the blonde woman said, her eyes popping wide. "We've been looking for you. There's a huge reward on your heads!"

The woman grabbed a tighter hold of Grian. He gulped and looked at Jeffrey. His friend was caught by the collar too, and his biker appeared even more fierce than Grian's.

The large man, who seemed to be the leader, glared at the boys and a wicked smile began playing round the edges of his lips. He was just about to say something, when suddenly the ground shook.

Grian wobbled sideways, knocking into the woman who held him. She dropped her hold.

The trees around them shivered from side to side and the remaining animals scampered for cover. Everything felt familiar, and Grian was overcome with fear. All of a sudden it made terrifying sense.

He was sure he knew what was about to happen next.

Memories clicked into place. Hansom had said, in the warehouse, that he was in a hurry to make the morning schedule; he wanted the Proctors to move out the phase-two boxes. The White Rose had written in his grandad's letter that *The sun will extinguish in phases, until only the embers are left.*

He willed himself to look skywards, though every sinew of his body worked against the impulse.

Grian's breath caught and he choked. Before his eyes another large chunk of light vanished from the sun, and now only a half of it shone bright. The morning darkened so much it almost seemed like night.

"Wow," the woman in the bandana gasped, staring up at the sky. "Ain't much left now. The Apocalypse is coming – what a time to be alive!"

Hoots, hollers and fist pumps raced through the crowd of bikers. They seemed to have forgotten Grian and Jeffrey, as the gang stared at the sun.

Just then Mushka's shaky voice rattled down Grian's EarPods.

"Guys, I know the sun's gone out again but I'm not dwelling on whatever move the BBEG is making right now, when we've got our own game to play. There's been a consensus on the hNet. They think they know where the White Rose is..."

"Where?" Jeffrey whispered.

Grian quickly looked around for a way to escape. The bikers were in awe gazing skywards. They weren't concentrating at all on the boys.

"They think she's in Quantum!" Mushka announced.

"What?!" Grian coughed surprised.

"That makes sense. Isn't Quantum where Yarrow said all de sun's energy disappeared de day of de earthquake, and also on de day de Tipping Point was wrecked?" Shelli said, jumping down out of the tree to land with a soft thud beside her friends. "Come on, de bikers are distracted. We need to sneak away before they remember you're still here!"

"Ah, Atlantis – Quantum – both lost cities. Quite obvious really, in retrospect," Jeffrey whispered, slipping quietly out of the clearing behind his friends.

"Hold on! Obvious!? Quantum! What? How?" Grian stuttered, confused. He stopped behind a tree a distance away from the bikers. "The White Rose can't be in Quantum – it was destroyed. There's an exclusion zone around it..."

"Yeah, but what if that's all lies?" Shelli said, turning to face him.

"But it's not lies. There's a huge dome covering the city – you can't fake that," Grian argued, his voice a little louder than he'd meant. "Dad drove past it once. Even from far off in the distance he said the dome's massive."

"No, I don't think de dome's a lie," Shelli whispered. "But what if – like Yarrow said in Dunstan – whatever we're told is going on inside it is? Anyway, come on, we've got to get going, those bikers will notice you're gone soon and come looking."

"Sooner than you think, young lady!" the leader of the bikers growled, stepping out from behind the tree. He grabbed the neck of Grian's jumper and lifted him up. "Now what is it you were so busy talking about that you didn't notice me coming?"

"Ahem, we, ahem…" Grian stuttered nervously.

"We were discussing how we are in dire need of transportation to Quantum if we've any chance of saving the world," Jeffrey stated, staring fearlessly at the man.

"Well, why didn't you just say so," the biker laughed, letting Grian go. "Cause now we're going there too. We came to help you fellas. I always knew Hansom was a creep before I even saw that viral video. If Armageddon is a-coming, we Riders of the Apocalypse won't go down without a fight! Hell – it's what we were founded for!"

CHAPTER 36

QUANTUM

Grian climbed onto the shiny metal bike and positioned himself on the back of the leather seat. The bike belonged to the leader of the gang, who was currently busy talking directions with his biker friends.

"Are you sure we should be going to Quantum? And with these people?" Grian whispered across to Shelli, who was sitting uncomfortably in the sidecar of another bike. Nach, who had perked up a little already, was curled in the seat beside her. "All we know so far is that maybe the White Rose is in Quantum. Is that really enough—"

"Time is running out, Grian!" Shelli nodded at the half dark sun.

"Precisely, Shelli," Jeffrey said, from the seat of

another bike, parked beside them. "Both the secret letter and the black mirror show we've to bring all the pieces of the puzzle to the White Rose. So if she is in Quantum, that's exactly where we need to be."

"But we don't have all the pieces to bring her!" Grian argued. "We don't even know what they all are!"

"No, but we have de crystal which is one piece. And of de three people de White Rose loves, we already know one of them is your grandad and—"

"And we've deduced the White Rose is Adabelle, Mother's sister," Jeffrey interrupted. "So perhaps with a little more investigation we can work out who the other two people are, even without Hansom's letter?"

"We're on de same page, Jeffrey," Shelli agreed.

"And I bet by the time you three get to Quantum, the hNet will have the rest of the riddle in the latest letter figured out, and we should know another piece of the puzzle," Mushka added, in their EarPods.

"But what if Hansom's letter is not about those three people at all and the hNet hasn't solved the latest puzzle? And what do we do when we get to Quantum? It's a no-go zone," Grian replied.

The engines around them roared to life, drowning out Grian's worries.

"Well, isn't this thrilling! Might as well enjoy the ride," Jeffrey cried over the sudden noise as he wrapped his arms around the biker lady in the red bandana, who'd just climbed onboard his bike.

"Are you ready?" the leader shouted at Grian over the engines.

The large man mounted his giant bike and grabbed the antler-like handlebars. Grian leaned forward and gripped tightly to the man's black leather jacket.

"Yes," Grian cried over the staggering noise, while the bike vibrated to life beneath him.

Despite his worries, he was ready, more ready than he had ever been. Mother told him before they left the Wilde forest that he should listen to his heart, not his head, and that she was brave once because she had to be, because there was no other choice.

Back then Grian didn't really understand her, but now he knew exactly what she meant.

His head told him what they were trying to do was impossible – they would never save the sun. The planet would die, so he should find Mam, Dad, Solas and Grandad and spend whatever time was left with them.

But his heart told him that against the odds three weird kids from Tallystick found each other and together uncovered the truth behind Hansom's web of lies.

It told him there was a movement growing. That, just like the bikers, people everywhere were waking up to the truth. It told him greed, money and power didn't have to win, and if they all pulled together there was hope – real hope for the future.

Over the howl of the engines, Grian's heart roared loud and clear. It told him he was brave but not just because he had to be any more.

Over the last few days his world was torn down, but behind it a new one was building. He'd seen the beauty of nature, he'd witnessed things he'd never dreamed possible and become part of something so much bigger than himself.

Grian was brave now because he wanted to be. He knew deep inside that he and his friends would save the world or they would die trying – because there were so many reasons to live.

THE END. FOR NOW...

CAN THE THREE YOUNG HEROES
SAVE THE THE WORLD
OR IS IT TOO LATE...?

Now people are beginning to believe that the sun is being stolen by tech-billionaire Howard Hansom and that he's been hoodwinking them all along.

But can Grian, Shelli and Jeffrey stop Hansom's despicable plan before the world is plunged into complete darkness?

Look out for the final roller-coaster adventure in **THE LIGHT THIEVES** series and read on for a sneak peek of what's to come

Grian, his two friends Jeffrey and Shelli and the leather-clad biker gang approached the hForest. Even from a distance the constant buzzing sound of the fake trees fizzled irritatingly in his head.

"I hate these places." Grian shivered stepping inside the tree line.

Crowds of angry people filled the forest all around them. Some carried flashlights illuminating their way round the digital trees in the densely packed space. Grian moved closer to Shelli who lit her Glimmer, making it easier to avoid collisions.

The crowd slowed when they came out the other side of the forest into the dark afternoon. Grian tried to peer ahead to what had caused the slowdown, but he was too small to see over the masses of people in front of him.

"What's going on?" he asked, when the crowd eventually stopped.

"Looks like we've reached the exclusion barrier around Quantum," the leader of the biker gang replied. "There are guards everywhere. They are not letting anyone through."

"I can't see anything," Grian said standing on his tippy toes to get a better look.

The large leather-clad man bent down and grabbed Grian, lifting him onto his broad shoulders.

"How's that?" he asked.

Grian was speechless and couldn't reply.

A distance in front of him, at the head of the crowd, was a digital glass wall. It looked a bit like the one in the Tipping Point, that had cordoned off the residential zone. The wall displayed warnings, like "Keep out" and "Exclusion zone" and "Anyone caught inside this barrier will be prosecuted". Armed guards patrolled on the other side of the wall. The guards wore black bulletproof vests like the ones Grian had seen in movies. They also had black gloves that looked suspiciously like Howard Hansom's powerful hThoughtTech.

But it wasn't the wall or the guards or even their weaponry that stole Grian's words. Way across a vast barren landscape behind the digital barrier was a huge glass dome hiding the city of Quantum. The dome reached skywards, reflecting the half dark sun on its curved glass panels. It was bigger than anything Grian could ever have imagined.

Someone near the front of the crowd pushed right up against the digital barrier and began to chant. It was a Tilt denier chant, the same chant Grian had heard his grandfather sing the day Howard Hansom arrived in Tallystick with his *PEOPLEPOWER* rally. That was the same day Solas, his sister, had run away to the Tipping Point and his grandad disappeared – it was the day Grian's life changed forever.

A sea of placards and banners started bobbing in the crowd as everyone began to join in the chant. Grian shivered reading the placards. Some said things like "Doomsday is Here" while others read "Billionaires Lie while We all Die" or "Howard is an evil Coward".

"Let us in," a woman screamed, banging so hard on the barrier that the stream of warning messages pixilated for a second. "We want to know the truth. What is happening to our sun? What are you doing inside that dome?"

The tension grew and people began throwing things at the glass barrier. To Grian's right, a group started slamming into the wall with some sort of battering ram.

The security guards seemed nervous. They linked arms behind the barrier and tried to look fearless facing the crowd.

Grian's heart pounded. The biker pulled him off his shoulders and left him back on the ground.

"You three get out of here," the bearded man said bending down to look the three friends in the eyes. "It's not safe here. Me and the gang are going up to help break down that wall. Hansom ain't keeping us out of Quantum any longer."

The crowd of bikers began to whoop and holler before pushing their way towards the front of the angry mob.

"We need to go," Grian said looking around.

"Yeah this crowd is going to blow," Shelli replied,

red-faced and a little panicked.

"I propose we pull back towards the hForest—" Jeffrey gasped just as the ground began to shake.

For a split second everything stopped, even the banging of the battering ram. Only the ground kept shaking.

Then the panic started. A group beside Grian, who were all wearing white, fell to their knees and began singing hallelujah at the top of their voices, while others in the crowd trampled over each other screaming as they ran in all directions.

"T-this can't be happening," Shelli stuttered, staring skywards.

Grian was about to reply when he was pushed to the ground. He'd just curled into a small ball to try to avoid being trampled when a huge gasp filled the area as though the crowd had taken one solitary breath.

He flipped around onto his back and stared at the sky. The day had plunged straight into the night as now three-quarters of the sun was dark.

ACKNOWLEDGEMENTS

I will keep this short and sweet. I'm never sure what to write each time it comes to the acknowledgements that won't be repetitive or bore you the reader – if in fact, you do read this page.

Luckily, my life is pretty consistent and mostly the people I want to thank are the same people I thank each time, except for a few. The few for this book are Lucas Maxwell, an amazing school librarian and all-around Dungeons and Dragons expert who generously lent me his knowledge and time to help make Mushka the DnD champion she is.

And Ava Thompson, whose aunt graciously gave to the Young Lives vs Cancer charity to have Ava's name inspire a character in this book.

And to those who are always by my side. Everyone at Usborne especially my editor Anne, who's done an amazing job five times now – thank you for your brilliant story mind. My agent Jordan for your sound sounding board. My writing group – I'm so glad we weathered a pandemic together and are still going strong and growing stronger. My friends for the walks and talks and general brain dumps, without your ears I'd sink in a sea of day-to-day worry. My family for your solid roots; with you I always have a place to come home.

To Robbie, my life's greatest adventure – you make every day exciting. To Jo and Bobbie for your eternal laughter and joy, my favourite thing to do is always with you.

And finally Mushka. Your courageous spirit worked its way into this story right under my nose and I am so glad that you did. You were a superstar who turned heads wherever you went. Loyal right to the end. You were the very best bestfriend.

USBORNE QUICKLINKS

Scan the code for links to websites where you can explore the history and science behind some of the ideas in this story, or go to usborne.com/Quicklinks and type in the title of this book.

Here are some of the things you can do at the websites we recommend:

- FIND OUT ABOUT THE SUN AND SOLAR POWER.
- DISCOVER WAYS TO FIGHT CLIMATE CHANGE.
- SEE ROBOTIC TECHNOLOGY INSPIRED BY NATURE.
- FIND OUT ABOUT JOHN DEE.
- ZOOM IN ON A SCRYING MIRROR USED BY AZTEC PRIESTS.

Children should be supervised online. Please follow the internet safety guidelines at Usborne Quicklinks.

To find out more about
HELENA DUGGAN and **THE LIGHT THIEVES**
go to **USBORNE.COM/FICTION**

 @USBORNE

 @USBORNE_BOOKS

@HELDIDEAS

#THELIGHTTHIEVES